A winter Night's Dream

also by andrew matthews

the flip side

A winter Night's Dream

Andrew Matthews

Delacorte Press

Published by Delacorte Press
an imprint of Random House Children's Books
a division of Random House, Inc.
New York

Originally published in Great Britain in 1997
by Mammoth, an imprint of Reed International Books Ltd.

visit us on the web! www.randomhouse.com/teens
educators and librarians, for a variety of teaching tools,
visit us at www.randomhouse.com/teachers

Library of Congress Cataloging-in-Publication Data
Matthews, Andrew.
A winter night's dream / Andrew Matthews.
p. cm.
Summary: Casey, a high school freshman, and Stew, a senior, search for love
separately, with the help of a favorite teacher, before meeting each other.
ISBN 0-385-73097-7 (trade) – ISBN 0-385-90127-5 (glb)
[1. Interpersonal relations—Fiction. 2. High schools—Fiction. 3. Teacher-
student relationships—Fiction. 4. Schools—Fiction.] I. Title.
PZ7.M43173Wi 2004
[Fic]—dc22
2003055290

The text of this book is set in 12-point Apollo.

Book design by Angela Carlino

Printed in the United States of America

July 2004

10 9 8 7 6 5 4 3 2 1

BVG

for Barbara, Hannah and Tony
and for Keren and Leigh

prologue

casey

I can't remember when this happened—maybe it was the summer before we started ninth grade—but, anyway, Helen and I were up in her bedroom listening to music when the conversation got around to boys. This wasn't surprising, because Helen's bedroom was like a shrine to males. She hadn't only stuck pictures of boy bands, TV actors and film stars over the walls; they were on the door, wardrobe and ceiling as well. Helen never took any pictures down, she just put new ones on top. I used to wonder if, underneath everything else, there were photos of kittens and ponies from the time before she was interested in blokes.

The most recent batch of pics featured guys wearing see-through tops, or no tops at all, so I said, "Are you into men, or flesh, Hel?"

Helen said, "Is there a difference?"

I said, "Sure! A cute guy with no brain is a real turnoff. What would your ideal man be like?"

Helen thought for a bit, then started pointing at the walls. "My ideal man would have his eyes, that one's mouth, hair like him, cute buns like that one over there, and—"

"Hang on!" I said. "You're talking about looks. I meant, what sort of *person* would your ideal man be?"

Helen shrugged. "I don't know . . . nice, I suppose."

I said, "Nice?"

"You know, sweet and considerate, and gentle, and shy . . ."

"Good with kids and handy at DIY? Oh, come on, Hel! You're talking Mr. Boring here!"

Helen went a bit sniffy on me when I said that. "All right," she said, "what would your ideal man be like, then?"

"Exciting," I said. "Different. A loner. A bit dangerous. Someone nobody else can handle."

"Sounds like the wolf in 'Little Red Riding Hood,'" Helen said.

Right away I got this picture in my mind. It was dark and I was riding a horse, galloping through a forest. The moon was shining and just in front of me I could see another rider, a man. I couldn't see his face, but I knew I had to follow him because he would lead me deeper and deeper into the forest, to the places no one else had ever been.

I though, Yeah! That's it!

"Of course," said Helen, "there's just one problem about an ideal man."

"What?"

"Finding him."

"I will," I said. "I'm not going to settle for second best."

"That's what everybody thinks," said Helen.

"But I'm not everybody. I'm me—and I mean it."

That talk with Helen stayed with me for a long time, much longer than a lot of sensible stuff I learned and instantly forgot. Funny how it goes, isn't it? One bit of conversation, or a film, or a book can completely change the way you look at things.

From then on I decided that things were going to change. I was going to stop being the person everybody else wanted me to be, so that I could become the person *I* wanted to be. When I had made my mind up, I felt great . . . then I started thinking about it.

Who the hell *did* I want to be?

act I scene I

when I found out mr. hart was going to teach me freshman english I was really pleased. He had this reputation for being really wacky, but he was a strict marker as well, so it was practically impossible to get A's from him. I'd seen him around school in his corduroy jacket and trousers, looking a bit like a creased teddy bear, and he'd taken a few assemblies that I actually listened to because they were funny, so I felt like I knew him.

But I started to have doubts when I was talking to Jonathan and Toby, who'd had Mr. Hart in seventh grade. I told them about how great I thought it was, having him for my teacher, and Jonathan shook his head. "I don't think you'll get on with him. He calls girls love and darling."

"Yeah," said Toby, "but he calls the boys love and darling as well."

So when I went into my first lesson with Mr. Hart, I got ready to meet a megaweird sexist perv.

We didn't get off to a brilliant start. Mr. Hart read out the class list and when he got to me he said, "Karen Celia Freeman?"

I said, "Casey."

Mr. Hart looked at me over the top of his glasses. "Sorry?" he said.

I said, "I'm called Casey. It's my initials—K.C. I don't like Karen or Celia. I don't answer to those names."

It came out sharper than I'd meant it to and I saw Mr. Hart wince, like he had me down as someone with attitude because I hadn't called him sir. There was this silence because the whole group was waiting to see what he was going to do about it.

"Celia . . . ," said Mr. Hart. "I once had a girlfriend called Celia. She used to say, 'Jolly dee!'"

The rest of the kids laughed, but I didn't. I thought Mr. Hart was putting me down, like all the other grown-ups in my life.

Being in the advanced class wasn't as good as I'd expected either. I mean, it was good in a way because if you said something intelligent you didn't get groans from the thickos at the back of the class, but it was harder to get top grades—and that meant pressure from Dad.

The main problem was Spanish. At the end of eighth grade, it seemed like a really good idea to opt for Spanish as a second language, but when it came to Spanish in ninth grade, I got lumbered with Mrs. Pereira. She was one of those teachers who can't keep control but carry on like there's nothing wrong. Kids would talk and mess around in her classes and she didn't do anything to stop them. She just chattered away at the front like everybody was paying attention. So, when report cards came along at the end of the Christmas term, I got a D in Spanish. I couldn't believe it. I'd never got lower than a C in my life. Mrs. Pereira's comment was "If Karen were to apply herself more to this subject, her grade would improve." I wanted to scribble on the bottom, "And if you applied yourself more to teaching, *all* our grades would improve." I didn't, because I knew I was going to get enough hassle as it was.

I don't want to make out like Dad was going to freak or anything, that's not his style. Dad goes in for the quietly-but-deeply-disappointed approach. When he got my report he flicked through it, going, "B, hey, that's all right!" Then he got to the D, and his mouth went all small and tight like a cat's bum. "So what's the problem with Spanish?" he said.

I said, "Mrs. Pereira's a rubbish teacher."

"If she was a rubbish teacher, she wouldn't have the advanced class, would she?" said Dad.

"She can't control us!"

"She shouldn't have to control you; you should be behaving yourself."

"I am!"

"Then how come you only got a D?"

He didn't go on and on at me. He just started talking about spending more time at work so I could have a private tutor. That made me feel like I'd let him and Mum down. The worst thing about that was, I knew Dad wasn't trying to make me feel guilty—I was doing it on my own.

That was typically Dad. When I was little he used to take me to the adventure playground. There was this big climbing frame that was meant for older kids, but I used to go on it. I'd climb a lot higher than I really wanted to, until it was actually scary. I'd glance down and Dad would be watching me with his Dad face on— like he was afraid for me but he was holding back from doing anything about it. I had to find out for myself that sometimes what I thought was a good idea was actually a big mistake. It's the best way to learn things, but it's also really, really hard.

My brother, Al, was his usual sympathetic self. I mean, whole seconds went by without him mentioning my bad grade. He was loving it that his big sis was in the doghouse and he didn't let me forget it. That night he had loads of chances, because practically every telly program had something about Spain or Spanish on it.

Come next morning, I wasn't feeling too brilliant about myself, especially since I got to school late for homeroom. Also, I'd lost the button off the left epaulet of my coat. The strap kept flopping and it was really irritating. On my way across the schoolyard, I met Mr. Hart coming the other way. He grinned at me and said, "Casey! How you doing?"

I said, "Crap!"

I got three paces past him before . . . Oh, my G-a-a-d! I just said "crap" to a teacher! I was sure Mr. Hart was going to report me to the principal, but it didn't happen. All day I kept to myself. I put up a CLOSED sign on my forehead and Rottweilered anyone who came near me—except Helen, but then Helen was a good enough mate to know when to leave me alone.

The weather didn't do much to improve things. The sky was gray, the ground was damp and the air felt like a slug crawling over my skin. I kept on remembering the rocky patch Mum and Dad had gone through when Dad was working so much we hardly saw him. He'd really tried to make it better—not going to so many conferences and leaving work earlier. Now he was going to start coming home late again so I could have a private tutor. That would means rows again, and the awful silences when Mum and Dad weren't talking—and it would be my fault.

By the time last lesson came—English—I felt like the pits. I didn't register much of the lesson, but every time someone laughed, I thought they were laughing about me. I went into this dark fantasy about me, Mum and Dad in the principal's office, and the principal saying, "I'm afraid her work really isn't up to scratch. I think she should be transferred to a less demanding section."

I don't know when I started crying. I heard this tapping noise, and when I looked down, I saw tears dropping onto my poetry book. When the bell went I didn't get out of my chair. I buried my face in a tissue like I was blowing my nose.

Helen said, "You coming?"

"In a minute. I'll catch you up."

When the last kid left the room I sighed with relief, because I was alone.

Only I wasn't. Mr. Hart was still there. He said, "Casey?"

I said, "It's all right, I'm fine."

"Of course you are," said Mr. Hart. "That's why you're crying. Silly me." Then, in a quieter voice, he said, "You can talk about it if you want to. If you want to tell me to push off and mind my own business, that's all right too."

"Look, I'm really sorry about what I said to you this morning, OK?"

"That's nothing to get upset about. If I worried about my pupils saying rude things to me, I'd be in the wrong job, wouldn't I?"

I laughed, and I was crying and laughing at the same time. Then words started coming out of me, and I couldn't stop them. I told Mr. Hart about Spanish, and Mum and Dad—the lot. Mr. Hart listened. He didn't even interrupt when I put down Mrs. Pereira.

When I'd finished, Mr. Hart said, "Your dad just wants the best for you. He cares about you. And stop worrying about your parents—they're not your responsibility. You've got your own life to live."

He said a lot of stuff about how he was glad he wasn't my age anymore. This was a bit of a shocker, because I'd always figured that teachers were twisted sods who envied young people their youth—it was the only explanation for school uniform. Mr. Hart seemed to understand what I was going through, and when he talked about it things made sense. More importantly, he made me laugh at myself until I felt better.

That was the first time I talked to Mr. Hart—I mean *really* talked, person to person instead of pupil to teacher. I'd never thought of teachers as people before.

scene II

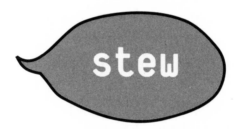

stew

It was a bad, bad day. I needed to talk to Mr. Hart, but when I found him after school he was with some skinny freshman girl. I could see that it would be tactless to interrupt, so I went home.

Some things you're fated to do alone.

I don't think I would have known what to say to him anyway, but at least he might have stopped me from feeling so pathetic. And I wasn't just *feeling* pathetic. I was Pathos itself, dressed in black, with a white mask for a face and swirling, moody violins in the background. When I got home I stuck my feet in the bath and ran cold water over them for fifteen minutes. I wanted a real pain to deal with.

It had all started with a ringing noise. I didn't know it was the tolling of the Bell of Doom—at the time I thought it was just the telephone. If I'd known, I would never have answered it, but I didn't, so I did.

It was Mr. Fletcher. "H-e-y, Stewart! Just the man I wanted to talk to!"

"Oh?" I said.

"How d'you fancy being lighting man for the dance concert?"

I didn't fancy it at all. I was a cool, sophisticated senior now. The last thing I needed was to get involved in anything to do with giggly little girls in tutus. But I had two problems, and they were both Mr. Fletcher. First off, I'd been his star pupil the previous year, and I would never have got an A in theater studies if he hadn't pushed me. Secondly, I'd had vague thoughts about wanting to be a teacher, and I'd been foolish enough to mention it to him.

I said, "W-e-e-l-l . . ."

"You're the only person I can depend on," said Mr. Fletcher, blackmailing me with "first off."

I said, "Ummm."

"Working with the kids will be good experience for you," he said, blackmailing me with "secondly."

12

I showed him what I was made of. I stood firmly on my own two feet and said, "Yeah, all right."

After all, it was only going to be an hour after school once a week, then a technical, a dress and the performance itself.

Most of the time after school I was up a gantry, slotting in gels and moving lights around. The rest of it was spent with the computer. Mr. Fletcher thought of himself as a whiz on computers, and he'd written his own software to control the lights. I think he had a dream of selling it to every drama department in the country and retiring on the proceeds.

The program was brilliantly thought out, with lots of unnecessary but impressive graphics. Unfortunately, it kept crashing, so we had to fall back on the old tried and tested setup, with Mr. Fletcher saying things like "Give me One to Nine, with just a splash of Fifteen!" while I pushed the faders up and down. As a concession to Mr. Fletcher's vision of himself as a New Technology Pioneer, these instructions were relayed over a radio mike and headsets. It was a bit pointless since Mr. Fletcher was sitting next to me in the lighting box, but teachers get a big touchy if you criticize their toys, don't they?

What with the lights, the gels and the Amazing Crashing Computer, I didn't actually get to see any dancing until the dress rehearsal. It was . . . well, pretty much what you'd expect from a school dance concert.

There was a "Me and My Shadow" routine, in which the shadow had been sucked through a hole in the fabric of time and emerged about two seconds out of sync with its partner. Next came a lovable Cockney barrow boys number involving a lot of kids bouncing up and down with their thumbs hooked in their suspenders. This was followed by a stylized street brawl, which had to be included because it was the only way Mr. Fletcher could get any boys to take part.

And then there was Lucy Dixon. "Lucy Dixon, Modern Dance," it said on my running sheet.

She knelt motionless on a single spot with her back to where the audience would be. She was wearing baggy white trousers and a pale blue top, studded with bits of mirror. When her music started she stood up and turned slowly, her hands held up to her face. Then the music changed and she lowered her hands, palms held out flat.

The cables holding my stomach snapped and it dropped thirty floors into the basement. Even from that distance I could see that Lucy's eyes were intensely blue. Her hair was a wonderful buttery gold. She looked so poised, and vulnerable, and gorgeous, that I missed my cue.

"Twenty-one to Twenty-seven," went Mr. Fletcher's voice in my earphones.

I said, "Uh?"

"Put some bleeding lights on, will you?" said Mr. Fletcher.

I did, and then I watched Lucy Dixon—although I suppose ate her with my eyes would be a more accurate description. She leapt and twirled, and made her body into shapes like breathing sculpture. Her hair was tied back in a ponytail and she used it like an extra limb. Sometimes she seemed able to turn air into invisible syrup, so that after a jump she could float gently down. And all the time, the mirrors in her top sent mad stars whirling around the drama studio walls.

At the end of her dance, I heard Mr. Fletcher chuckle and mutter, "That's my girl!"

I stared hard at Lucy Dixon and wished that I could say the same thing.

After the rehearsal, I scrambled down the lighting-box ladder into the Gents and then went out into the corridor. A lot of little kids passed me on their way out and gave me funny looks because I was loitering so obviously. Then Lucy emerged from the greenroom.

I'd been expecting her to be a disappointment close-up—a face full of zits, or with a squint, or something—but she wasn't. She'd untied her hair so that it flowed, and her eyes were like blue Turkish delight. She was talking to a friend and didn't notice me. As she passed I said, "Cool dance!" I ought to have prefaced it with,

"Yo, dude!" and made myself sound like a complete idiot instead of only going halfway.

Lucy turned as though she were still dancing. "Thank you!" she said, and smiled. "See you tomorrow!"

Even after she'd gone, I could still see her smile.

I lurched along the corridor and went through the doors into the drama studio. Mr. Fletcher was there, checking through the program with the front-of-house manager.

"Tina Jeffries?" said the manager.

"Eight Purple North," said Mr. Fletcher.

"Lucy Dixon?"

"Ten Green West," Mr. Fletcher said.

I thought, ARGH! NO!

It isn't actually carved in stone that if thou art a senior thou shalt not go out with girls younger than sophomores, but if you tried it in our school, people would start whispering and giggling behind your back.

As I walked home I shrugged and tried to forget about Lucy Dixon, but in order to do it, I had to think about her so that I could remember what it was I had to forget.

I would have been all right if I hadn't dreamt about her. It wasn't a horny dream—it was far, far worse than that. I dreamt I was walking over to the senior lounge when Lucy came running up to me. She smiled and grabbed hold of my hand. All the kids going past stopped to goggle and I got really embarrassed, but Lucy said, "Who cares?"

I said, "I do, I care about you."

And when I woke up, I was still saying it.

I couldn't lie to myself then, because it was obvious: I'd developed an instant crush on a girl I didn't know, and who didn't know me. If I tried to get to know her better, I was going to make myself look ridiculous and I was going to get talked about. On the other hand, there was this big, aching space where my insides used to be. And after the concert she might disappear back into the fifteen hundred other kids at school and I'd never see her again. I wanted to discuss it with someone, and I knew that my mates would laugh in my face.

What I really needed to do was talk to Mr. Hart.

scene III

on the last Monday of term, Helen and I had lunch on one of the concrete benches by the tennis courts—strictly against school rules, but hey, we were ninth-grade rebels, right? Helen opened her lunch box and took out a stick of celery and a piece of cheese that was so small it looked like someone had got it out of a mouse's eye with the corner of a hanky.

I said, "Great lunch, Hel."

Helen said, "It's for my zits."

"But you don't have any zits. Your complexion is so perfect that I hate you for it."

"Ah, but I might be asked to a lot of parties this Christmas, and I just know that if I'm going to get a zit, it'll be on the morning of a party, so I'm taking precautions."

"Good idea. Now you only have to worry about fainting from hunger."

Helen always worried about things—in fact, there was no known solution to which she couldn't find a problem. If Helen had nothing to worry about, it really worried her. She frowned at me and said, "You reckon?"

I said, "Uh-oh!" I didn't say it because of Helen, I said it because I noticed Terry Melton and Lee Pace coming our way.

Helen turned to see what I was going "Uh-oh!" about, and she went "Uh-oh!"

Terry and Lee were walking the way they usually did, by pushing each other and laughing a lot.

Helen said, "Why do they do that?"

I said, "Boys can't hug the way girls can, so they punch each other and arm-wrestle instead. Also, they're incredibly stupid."

Terry and Lee clocked us, whispered a bit and then elbowed each other in a go-on-no-you sort of way.

I said, "Prepare to repel boarders!"

They came over to us. Terry casually rested one foot

on the end of the bench and leant on his knee. He said, "Hey, it's Casey and Helen!"

I said, "Yes, and this is a bench, that's the tennis courts, and those big things on the lawn over there are trees."

Terry laughed and shook his head. "She cracks me up!" he said to Lee. "Every time I talk to this girl, she cracks me up."

"Stick around," I said, "maybe I can get you to fall apart completely."

Terry jerked his shoulders like the muscles in his arms were too big for his school pullover, but they were nowhere as big as the muscles in his head. He said, "Me and Lee was just thinking."

I said, "You like a challenge, then? Will you carry on doing it, or has the novelty worn off?"

Terry said, "Nah, look, seriously—how about coming to the Christmas disco with us?"

"Yeah!" said Lee, who was standing over Helen the way the Empire State Building stands over New York.

Obviously, anyone who asks a freshman girl to a school disco is a Deeply Sad Person, and I had to stop myself from giggling—but Helen was getting panicky. Her eyes were jumping about like gerbils.

"I don't think so," I said.

Terry said, "Oh, come on. I got some weed. We could smoke up before we go. Be a great laugh."

I said, "Get stoned and go to a school dance? That's a bit of a waste, isn't it?"

Terry gave me this leering look. "Don't have to go to the dance," he said. "We could get mellowed out and then do whatever."

"Yeah!" said Lee. "Burger King!"

I said, "No."

"Eh?" said Terry. "How d'you mean, no?"

I said, "I mean no as in, not yes."

Terry blinked at me. He couldn't believe any girl in her right mind would turn him down, so he decided I wasn't in my right mind. "Come on, Lee," he said. "These two must be frigid!"

They walked off, pushing each other.

I wanted to say something to Helen, but she was hyperventilating. Her breathing sounded like a hacksaw cutting through a copper pipe.

"Not *again*, Hel!"

"So . . . rry," Helen said. She could only say one syllable at a time and it was like listening to a little kid learning how to read.

"Where's your paper bag?"

Helen took it out of her lunch box. It was the same sixties flowery bag she'd used last time. She breathed into the bag and it went up and down. It reminded me of one of those rubber things patients breathe into when they're having an operation.

I said, "What brought this on, Terry and Lee?"

"No," said Helen. "My . . . bum."

"What's wrong with your bum?"

"Every . . . thing."

While I was waiting for Helen's breathing to get back to normal, I tried to work out what she meant. I mean, I don't have any figure to speak of, but Helen does. I know, because I've heard guys speak of it.

"I saw it in the bathroom mirror this morning," said Helen. "It's huge!"

I said, "What, the mirror?"

"My bum. It's epic. How can I go to any parties with it?"

"Well, you can't go without it, can you? Anyway, there's nothing wrong with it."

"Isn't there?"

"Hell, it's a bum to die for."

Helen brightened up after that, just about the same time that I started to feel down. Terry and Lee reminded me of how long it had been since I'd been out with anybody.

The summer before, I'd had this thing with Ryan Wallis. Ryan was a year older than me, so going out with him was a Big Deal—plus, he was gorgeous. Only . . . it turned out to be a real letdown. I trusted Ryan with my feelings, and he did to me what a shredder does to hedge trimmings.

So I was a bit off boys. All the nice ones were taken, or too old, or the available ones were nerds, dogs or sharks, like Terry and Lee. The problem was, if I didn't have a boyfriend, people would wonder what was wrong with me. Including me.

Helen and I went to registration, and then it was English. We'd prepared a poem to discuss. Mr. Hart made it obvious he wasn't going to let us be last-Monday-of-term-ish, because when he came in he went "Right!" in his teacher's voice.

Mr. Hart doesn't believe in taking prisoners. There are no hands-up; he asks people questions straight, and if you try to ignore him, he won't go away. He says things like "Come along! Let's prove that there *is* life before death."

He asked me a question, and I went for it. I told him what I thought, and it was *me* telling *him*, not Casey Freeman telling Mr. Hart.

And then I said, "I don't get the love stuff."

Mr. Hart said, "What?"

"I don't see how the bit about love is supposed to fit in with the rest."

There was a murmur of agreement around me.

Then Mr. Hart went for it. He exploded into words, most of which got past me before I could check them out. What it came down to was that the love stuff was the whole point of the poem.

I said, "But how were we supposed to know that? We're only a bunch of kids—most of us haven't had a relationship yet!"

Mr. Hart said, "Then it's time you did."

I went, "Huh?"

"Go out and fall in love with somebody!" said Mr. Hart. "It'll do your understanding of literature the world of good."

The others laughed and was I embarrassed, or what? My toenails carved half-moons in my insoles.

As I was leaving the lesson I said to Mr. Hart, "Were you being wacky or serious?"

"When?" said Mr. Hart.

"When you said that thing about falling in love."

"Wacky-serious," said Mr. Hart.

"What if I'm not ready to fall in love yet?"

"Who is? Falling in love isn't something people do when they feel ready—it happens to them. Ready or not, here comes love!"

"You make it sound like an accident."

Mr. Hart said, "Now you're getting it!"

But I wasn't; all I was getting was depressed.

scene IV

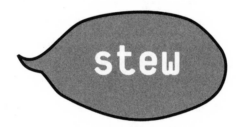

As usual, I called for Phil on Monday morning and, as usual, he wasn't quite ready. He came out of his front door trying to eat a piece of toast and put his jacket on at the same time, and he nearly went flying down the porch steps.

"Are you OK?" I said.

"Sure," said Phil. "I wake up at eight, but I don't get coordinated until nine."

We didn't say anything until we turned onto Crispin Street. Then Phil announced a game of Barf Bag by making an unexpected first move. He said, "A glass of Coke and a mayonnaise sandwich."

"That was a bit below the belt!" I said. "A cup of espresso with a cheese-and-chutney toastie."

Phil smirked as though he really had me this time. "Tomato soup and a pink-iced bun," he said.

I wasn't really in the mood and I could have let him win, but Barf Bag is a matter of honor. I said, "A bar of chocolate and a pint of warm Camembert."

"Barf Bag!" said Phil, with the obligatory retching groans. "How come you're so hot at this game?"

I said, "Because you're as thick as two short planks and I'm a master of sparkling wit and repartee. Phil, d'you believe in love at first sight?"

Phil glared at me. "What kind of question is that to ask first thing on a Monday morning? No, I don't."

I said, "Why not?"

"Take a look around," said Phil.

I did. The houses on Crispin Street looked sleazy and dank; front gardens were filled with half-rotten plants; trash bags were lined up at the curb and a couple of them had been disemboweled by cats; a piece of soiled tissue paper waved at me from the gutter.

"Point taken," I said.

Phil said, "Why are you such a hopeless romantic?"

"Someone has to be," I told him. "We're the generation that's had everything explained to us—AIDS, condoms—it's all so . . ."

"Yucky?" said Phil.

"Clinical," I said.

"Of course it's clinical, it's biology! So who is it this time?"

"Hey?"

"Who are you in love with now?"

"I was being theoretical."

"No you weren't!" said Phil. "You don't get theoretical, you get moonstruck! Remember Pippa Hardcastle?"

I said, "I was just a kid then."

"And now you're a broken-down old man of seventeen," said Phil. "And what about that girl you got the hots for last summer, the one who worked on the checkout at the supermarket? How many cans of Coke did you end up buying?"

"It was the only way I could make contact!"

"But you didn't make contact! You just flopped about like a cold bread-and-butter pudding!"

"It wasn't my fault," I said. "When you're standing in a supermarket queue, it's difficult to find the right moment to tell the girl behind the register that her eyes are brighter than the morning star!"

"Pree-cisely," Phil said. "That's why being romantic won't work, because there'll never be a right time or place! You only fall in love with the unobtainable. You always have, ever since you had that thing about that weather forecaster."

I said, "I can dream, can't I?"

"You don't do anything *but* dream, mate! It's time you faced reality."

We were on Chestnut Drive by this time, and I noticed Garganzo on the corner, smoking a hand-rolled cigarette. Garganzo's real name is Alan Wethered, but he's big enough for Garganzo to suit him better. As Phil and I approached, Garganzo broke wind loudly, but he didn't do it in a personal way.

Phil said, "What's up, Garg? On your way to school?"

"Is it Monday?" said Garganzo.

"'Fraid so," said Phil.

"Think I'll give it a miss. Can't seem to get me head round Mondays. Maths and that." Then his face split into a wide, dreamy grin. "You going to Fozzer's party Saturday?"

Phil said, "Probably."

"I am, definitely," said Garganzo. "I'm gonna get completely off my face."

The thought of Garganzo off his face was awesome, and it occupied my mind for the rest of Chestnut Drive.

Phil said, "There you go, your big chance!"

"What is?" I said.

"Fozzer's party," said Phil. "Come along and get real."

"I haven't been invited."

"Don't talk daft! No one gets *invited* to Fozzer's parties!"

I didn't give the party an awful lot of thought, because I was too busy thinking about the dance concert that evening.

It was due to start at seven o'clock, but I turned up at five-thirty. I was hoping that I could somehow ground the energy that was building up inside me. I wandered through the greenroom, listening to the silence and imagining how noisy it would be later, when the kids arrived. On the table next to the racks of costumes were two plastic cups filled with safety pins and bits of elastic. I could feel myself getting nostalgic about the concert before it was even over.

I drifted into the drama studio. It looked dim with just the houselights on. There were pieces of white tape on the floor to mark where the scenery went, and they were already grubby and peeling. I noticed how tacky the drama studio was. Some of the seating was ripped and the gangways had been scuffed by thousands of composite soles. At the end of the Christmas production the back wall had been painted white in such a hurry that the towers of Oz still showed through.

It was unbelievably depressing.

And then the doors of the drama studio opened, like a bird flapping its wings, and Lucy Dixon bounced in. She was wearing a dark blue coat and had a bag slung over her left shoulder. As soon as she saw me she smiled, and it was like someone had turned all the faders up full. "Hello, lighting man!" she said.

"Hello, star!" I said, and my voice sounded peculiar because of the lump in my throat.

"You must be keen, being here so early," said Lucy.

"Just a few last-minute checks," I said. "How about you?"

"I came to warm up."

She shrugged off her bag and coat in one smooth movement. Underneath, she was wearing a loose yellow shirt and blue jeans. She walked across the studio floor like a dancer, putting one foot precisely in front of the other; then she spun round on one foot and practiced a bow. "I love being in a theater before a show," she said. "You can feel the magic beginning."

"Magic?"

"When the lights go down, and everything's quiet, and the spot goes on, you can feel everybody looking at you. If you dance well, you can make them forget all their problems. It's magic!"

"And then, afterward, you have to go back to reality," I said.

"Not me," Lucy said softly, looking round. "This is what's real."

"Hey, you're a bit of a romantic, aren't you?"

Lucy said, "I'm a dancer," as if it explained everything.

I got a peculiar prickling sensation at the back of my neck. I felt as though Lucy had given me a glimpse of who she really was, and I wanted to tell her who I was in return. Right that moment, I thought I could do it, without thinking too much first or fumbling the words. . . .

And then Mr. Fletcher burst in, rubbing his hands together so they squeaked. "Right, guys and gals!" he said briskly. "It's nearly bums-on-seat time!"

So much for magic . . .

scene v

on the last day of term some joker had the amaz-
ingly original idea of setting off the fire alarm.
Oh, how we laughed as we trooped out on the playing
field and the wind froze our butts off. When we were
all lined up, I said to Helen, "So, are we going to
Fozzer's party on Saturday, or not?"

Helen went dark and doubtful. "I don't know," she
said. "I'm not sure my parents will . . . I mean . . ."

I said, "Fozzer."

"Right," said Helen.

Fozzer's reputation was so famous even Helen's parents had heard of him. Everybody had. I bet that if we ever make contact with extraterrestrial civilizations the first question they'll ask will be, "Is it true about Fozzer?"

"So lie," I said.

"I can't! You know how useless I am at it! My dad will catch me straightaway!"

"We're talking party time, Hel! Are you going to let a trivial little thing like your parents stand in your way?"

"I'll work on them," said Helen. "How about your parents?"

"Not a problem," I said. Meanwhile I was thinking, How the hell do I talk them into this one?

My parents were clever. I mean, they actually *learnt* stuff. Once upon a time I'd been able to use the old "Da-ad, Mum says if you say it's all right with you . . ." quickly followed by "Mu-um, Dad says if you say it's all right, then I can . . ." but they'd figured that one out by the time I was thirteen.

As I was going back into school, thinking about this, I saw Mr. Hart. I thought, Aha! He'll know how I should approach Mum and Dad.

Only he was talking to a senior, so I couldn't ask him. I shouted, "Merry Christmas, Mr. Hart!"

He looked round and shouted, "Merry heart, Miss Christmas!"

Helen said, "What did he say that for?"

"No particular reason."

"He's weird!"

"No, he's not! Mr. Hart's cool!"

When I got home the telly was on. American voices jabbered in the sitting room, so I guessed Al was in. I looked round the door and said, "Hello, Mr. Mature. Watching the cartoons?"

Al said, "Bog off, butt-face!"

Mum came in not long after and I helped get dinner ready. I figured that if we were working together I could casually mention that there was this party I fancied going to, but Mum wasn't in an approachable mood. Someone at work had got right up her nostrils, and while she was telling me about it, she was chopping up carrots like they were this person's fingers.

This was the moment Al chose to slouch against the kitchen door and go, "When's dinner going to be ready? I'm starving!"

Mum slammed down her knife and had a right go at him about his attitude. Al shifted into top whine gear, saying how everything in the house revolved around me, and how he didn't see the point in having been born, since he was so obviously in the way. I told him what a good laugh that was, and while the three of us were talking at each other, Dad came in.

He said, "That's what I like to see, family harmony!"

Mum waved to him but didn't stop talking.

Dad said, "Hello, dear, hard day at work? Well, not so bad, considering. Would you like a cup of tea? Hmm, love one!"

He waded past everybody and filled the kettle, listening to me tell Al what a spoilt brat he was and nodding in approval. When there was a word-sized gap in my voice, Dad said, "Maybe you'll have better luck when the new baby arrives. Perhaps it'll be a little sister for you."

There was an explosion of silence. I looked at Al, he looked at me, we both looked at Mum and then we all looked at Dad. I said, "Oh, *wh-a-a-t!* You haven't? I mean, you mean . . ."

"Grr-oss!" said Al.

Mum said, "I haven't got the faintest idea what he's talking about."

"See?" said Dad, smiling at Al and me. "Things could be a lot worse, so be happy with the way they are."

I said, "But . . . !"

Dad said, "No."

Al said, "It wasn't . . . !"

"Definitely not," said Dad. "And if either of you says another word, it's death by plastic fork."

It was no use talking to my parents while their blood sugar level was low, so I waited until after dinner. Al went up to his room to listen to Death Thrash Metal and look at the magazine he kept hidden under his mattress, and I had the folks to myself.

I said, "Oh, yeah, there's a party on Saturday night. Can I go?"

Dad said, "Party?"

"Yes," I said. "You know, young people having a good time together? Remember?"

Mum said, "Whose party?"

"Some guy at school's. What's the matter, don't you trust me or something?"

"There's parties, and there's *parties*," said Dad.

"I don't think they'll be serving tea and cucumber sandwiches, but it'll be cool. I can take care of myself."

"I don't know . . . ," said Mum.

"Are you afraid you didn't bring me up right?"

"You will be, er . . . ," said Dad. "I mean, you won't go . . ."

"Spit it out!"

Dad pulled his Dad face and said, "You will be sensible, won't you?"

"Do *you* go to parties to be sensible?"

I'd got him there, because the Christmas before he'd come home so stinko from the office party, they had to pour him out of the taxi.

Dad sighed and said, "Ten-thirty."

I said, "Eleven-thirty."

Dad said, "Eleven."

"Done!" I said.

And that was it; quite easy, really. I don't know why I hadn't thought of laying a guilt trip on my parents before—after all, they'd been doing it to me for years.

Before I went to bed, I had a mirror-think. I sat in front of the wardrobe mirror, looked at myself and wondered what to wear on Saturday. I knew the girl in the mirror was me, but who was that?

Who to be, who to be?

I decided grunge-me. The Doc Martens I'd painted daisies on were a definite, and the thrift-shop leather jacket. Then a longish skirt with black leggings, a blouse half hanging out and a shapeless sweater. All that was wrong was the zits. I didn't have any, and the whole grunge thing looked better if you had zits—but there you go, nobody's perfect.

I shouldn't have started mirror-thinking because it got me onto myself. Was I going to spend the rest of my life looking into mirrors on my own? I wondered where *he* was, the guy who was going to hit me like a tidal wave and sweep me away to growing up. If I knew where he lived, I'd send him a postcard with "Wish you were here" written on it.

I thought, Maybe the party.

You can never tell with parties, can you?

scene VI

stew

The fire alarm went right in the middle of Henry VIII's foreign policy. Miss Bowater rolled her eyes and groaned, and the history group groaned too, but we were grateful for the interruption. One of the disadvantages of being in the twelfth grade is that at the end of the term you don't get word searches and quiz games—the teachers make you work.

I said to Phil, "This is probably a symbolic, anti-social act carried out by a disaffected misfit."

"Really?" said Phil. "I thought it was just some idiot mucking around."

There were fifteen hundred kids outside, all moving in the same direction.

"This is such a hassle!" said Phil. "Why don't they just leave us alone and let us fry?"

I said, "Hmm," because I wasn't listening. I was scanning the crowds, hoping to see Lucy. No such luck, but I did spot Mr. Hart checking through his class list. "It's now or never," I said.

"What is?" said Phil.

"Talking to Mr. Hart," I said.

I waited until people starting filing back in, and then I approached Mr. Hart. The playing field isn't the ideal place for a conversation, but I didn't have much choice.

Mr. Hart said, "Stewart! How's the twelfth grade treating you?"

I said, "Fine."

"What are you doing in English?" said Mr. Hart.

"*King Lear.* Mr. Hart, if you idolize somebody d'you think it's better to keep quiet about it or tell them? Because if you tell them and they laugh at you, you know they're not perfect and you don't idolize them anymore. But if you keep quiet they won't know, and then you keep wondering what might have happened if you hadn't."

"Hang on, Stewart, was there a question in there somewhere?"

39

"Sort of."

Mr. Hart looked at me closely. "You're in love again," he said.

It was no use pretending—I'd talked to Mr. Hart often enough for him to know me. I said, "Not yet, but I'm thinking about it."

"You can think too much about things, Stewart. You can think your whole life out of the window."

"There's this girl . . ."

"That much I intuited," said Mr. Hart.

"She's incredibly beautiful, and she's absolutely perfect, only . . . she's younger than I am."

"How much younger?"

"Ninth grade."

I could see Mr. Hart thinking it through, working out where the problems were. As he was doing it, someone shouted to him, and he turned to shout back.

I said, "I'm just being stupid, aren't I? It's crazy! I should forget the whole thing and get myself a life, right?"

Mr. Hart said, "Ask her out."

"What?"

"Walk straight up to her and say, 'Would you like to go out with me?'"

"It's not that easy! What are people going to say when they see a senior chatting up a freshman girl?"

"Look, Stew," said Mr. Hart, "you can either live

your life according to what other people will say about you or you can do what you want. Anyway, what makes you think you're so important? I'm sure people have got a lot of other things to talk about."

That made me stop and think. "What if she says no?"

"Then you'll know she's not interested, so you can stop wasting your time," said Mr. Hart.

That made me think too.

"And by the way," said Mr. Hart, "this girl, whoever she is, isn't perfect."

"How d'you know?"

"Because no one is."

There was hardly anybody left on the field. I suddenly felt conspicuous standing there. I said, "I'll remember. Thanks for the chat."

"Anytime," said Mr. Hart.

And I went back to Henry VIII. I was feeling pretty optimistic. Mr. Hart had convinced me that the Lucy situation was straightforward.

Then it struck me: It was the end of term; how could I ask Lucy out when I wasn't going to see her until after Christmas? If I had to wait two and a half weeks, I was bound to chicken out.

Inside my head, a brief sunny interval was followed by an area of deep depression, bringing prolonged showers of misery.

On the way home, Phil said, "OK, I can't stand the silence anymore! Out with it, who is this girl anyway?"

"What girl?"

"Come off it, Stew!"

"Someone who might fit."

"Come again?"

"Personalities are like pieces of a jigsaw puzzle," I said. "My personality is a different shape to everyone else's, but out there somewhere is another personality that will fit mine. All our wiggly bits will go together."

Phil said, "You're in love with a girl who looks like a piece of *jigsaw puzzle*? You've totally flipped, mate. You ought to take a little advice from Dr. Phil."

"Which is?"

"Come to Fozzer's party, drink lots of alcohol and get a little out of it."

"Will it help?"

Phil shrugged. "Who knows? You can never tell with parties."

ACT II **scene I**

You could tell which was Fozzer's house from the far end of the street. All the other houses were tidy and respectable, with light from televisions flickering over the drawn curtains. Fozzer's house was bright, and you could feel the music from it pulsing in your stomach before your ears heard it.

"So remember," Helen said, "if my parents ask you, we went to that film at the Royal."

"When are your parents going to ask me?"

"I don't know! They might ring you up or something."

"Why would they do that? Relax, will you? Stop being so paranoid."

"D'you really think I'm paranoid?"

"No," I said. "But I tell other people you are, behind your back."

The first person we met was Alby. He was down on his hands and knees on this patch of grass in front of the house, and he was hurling.

I said, "Hi, Alb!"

Alby raised a hand and between heaves said, "Case!"

The front door was open, and Julie Marshall and Eddy Coker were in the hall. It was difficult to work out where Eddy ended and Julie began.

"I didn't know you could do that standing up," Helen said to me.

"It's the first time anyone's tried it," I said.

There were people everywhere, dancing, drinking, snogging. They were sitting on the floor or the stairs and some were practically dangling from the banisters. They all looked like they were having the good time they'd made up their minds to have. I wanted a good time too, and I wondered where it was.

Helen and I went into the kitchen to deposit our contribution—some Belgian lager. Garganzo was in one corner, fisting potato chips into his face from a stainless steel bowl. In the middle of the kitchen stood Fozzer himself.

He was wearing a dinner jacket, flowery shorts, red sneakers and two girls. One was under his left armpit and the other was draped round his neck. I think they were holding him upright. The three of them swayed from side to side, like a pub sign in the wind.

Fozzer grinned and said, "Good evening! So good of you to come. Drinks in the kitchen, dancing in the living room, drugs in the front bedroom." Fozzer's voice was sort of raspy and posh, like the voice of a butler in an old film, and he wasn't putting it on—he really talked like that.

I said, "Oh, wow!"

Fozzer squinted at me and frowned. "Did you just say 'Oh, wow'?" he said.

"Er . . . yes."

"How charming! Are you drunk yet?"

"I've only just arrived."

"That's no excuse," said Fozzer. He looked at the two girls. "To the bathroom, ladies. Ready. . . set . . . go!"

They staggered across the kitchen like they were in a three-legged race.

I said, "Are you all right?"

"Never finer!" said Fozzer. "It's just my legs. They always get drunk first."

"You're going to have a stonking hangover in the morning."

"Only if I get sober," Fozzer said.

I poured myself a glass of something red and took a swig. It tasted of mouthwash and petrol and, after my breath came back, I said to Helen, "All right, party animal, let's go dance!"

In the living room, people were going up and down like they were boiling in a saucepan. There wasn't a lot of room, but Helen and I found a space and I let myself go.

I danced me. I went right off into another place where my arms and legs turned into music. I could see myself on this big chessboard thing and all the people I knew were frozen onto squares. I was the only one moving, because I was the only one who knew how to move.

For a long time, that was it—drinking and dancing, followed by more drinking and dancing. Guys joined in the dancing every now and then, but I didn't pay much attention to them. Then I paid a lot of attention because a slow song started and this guy grabbed me. Suddenly—*whump!*—I was in a clinch with a gorilla.

I said, "Er . . ."

A voice in my ear said, "You're just so . . ."

He was stuck to me like a wet raincoat and his breath smelt of ashtrays. I wasn't dancing anymore, I was drowning.

Then another voice said, "Excuse me, pal. The young lady's with me."

It wasn't a loud voice, but it sounded kind of dangerous. The gorilla let go of me and I turned to see who my rescuer was, and monsters ate my brain.

His hair was long and black with yellow streaks dyed in it—the kind of hair it takes a lot of nerve to walk round with. His eyes were this really amazing color, the same as slates in the rain. And he had cheekbones, major cheekbones that supermodels would kill for. They made him look like an Aztec chief or something. I was in danger of melting into a gooey puddle and disappearing down a crack in the floorboards.

The gorilla curled up his top lip, trying to look hard, and said, "I was only dancing with her, wasn't I?"

Mr. Hottie said, "Well, you're not now. Why don't you go and find someone else to dance with?"

"Gonna make me?" the gorilla said.

"I won't have to," said Mr. Hottie, "because you're going to get really intelligent and just walk away while you still can." His voice was soft, like he didn't have to shout to make his point, and his eyes were really menacing, staring straight ahead without blinking.

The gorilla looked scared, like he'd got himself into a situation that was completely out of hand. I thought there was going to be a fight and so did the gorilla, only he knew it was a fight he couldn't win. He held up his hands. "Sorry, mate!" he said, and backed off.

When he was safely out of the way, I turned to Mr. Hottie and said, "Thanks a lot."

He didn't look at me; he was still drilling the gorilla with his eyes. "I've had my eyes on that guy ever since he got here," he said. "It's always the mouthy ones who cause trouble."

"D'you always go to parties expecting trouble?"

Mr. Hottie shrugged. "D'you want me to make him apologize to you?"

"Hey, no, look, it's all right!" I shook my arms and legs. "I've still got all the bits that I came in with." I smiled at him. "I don't know you, do I? I'm Casey."

"I'm Dean. Are you sure you're all right? You look a bit . . ."

I was feeling a bit . . . My stomach started turning over like the drum of a washing machine. I said, "I think I may puke."

"Come on," said Dean. "I'll take you outside for some fresh air."

We tiptoed through the people in the hall and kitchen and went into the back garden. It was a clear night. Millions of stars were out and the moon was really low.

"Try not to think about it," said Dean. "Talk about something that'll take your mind off it."

"All right. D'you live round here?"

"Yeah, but I haven't been here long. I've been living in Spain."

"You don't look Spanish."

"My family and I were over there for a year. I grew up that year. It taught me a lot."

He talked about it. His dad had lost his job, and some property dealer had talked him into investing his severance pay in Spanish holiday villas. The family went to Spain to live, but the deal turned out to be a complete rip-off.

"We lost everything," said Dean. "Dad spent months trying to get the money, but it didn't do any good. We had to beg the return fare to the U.K. from the British Consulate. We used to be a close family at one time, but now . . ."

He told me what it had done to his family, and his voice was cold. He said some pretty cruel things about his parents, but as he was saying them, I got the idea that he was covering up how much he was hurt.

"Hey, you didn't come here to listen to this!" he said. "You must be bored rigid."

"No, I'm not," I said.

"That's what you get for being easy to talk to," said Dean.

It was just an offhand compliment, but I put it away carefully because I knew I'd want to look at it again later.

And then, just when everything was really looking promising, the alarm on my watch went off.

"Oops!"

"What is it?" said Dean.

"I've got to go, otherwise I'll get grounded."

I didn't want to leave, and I thought Dean didn't want me to leave either, because his wet-slate eyes went disappointed just for a second; then he blinked really slowly. "Well, it was good talking to you," he said.

"Me, too. Bye."

Just as I got to the kitchen door, I turned and said, "Maybe we should have another talk sometime."

"D'you really mean that or are you just saying it?" Dean said.

"I never just say things."

It took ages to find Helen. By the time we left Fozzer's, we had to walk fast.

"Where did you disappear to?" said Helen.

"I was talking to some guy in the garden."

"Was he nice?" said Helen.

"He was grotesquely hideous. I only talked to him out of pity."

"Are you trying to wind me up?"

"No, I'm succeeding in winding you up."

"But *was* he nice?"

"Sex on legs, Hel," I said. "He says he wants to talk to me again, and—*oh, crap!*"

"What's wrong?" said Helen.

"I didn't give him my phone number! He doesn't know where I live! He doesn't even know my second name!" I could hear myself tearing in two. I wanted to run back to Fozzer's and find Dean, but if I did I'd be late, and Mum and Dad would ground me for the rest of the holiday. "Oh, no! What am I going to do?"

"Love will find a way," said Helen.

I said, "How?"

"I don't know," said Helen. "I just said it to make you feel better."

"Hey, you know what, Hel? It didn't work."

parties. I've never actually liked them very much because I don't have a herd instinct. I remember my parents taking me to puppet shows and when all the other children shouted out to the puppets, I didn't, not because I didn't want to—I just couldn't.

Something gets into people at parties and makes them do incredibly stupid things that they wouldn't normally even dream of doing. Part of this is due to the influence of alcohol, but it's mostly the Party Thing. You can see it in people's eyes just before they turn into Godzilla. I've never been able to catch it myself.

Despite all this, I went to Fozzer's party with Phil, but I dressed in black so that everyone would know that I wasn't enjoying myself.

On the way, I said, "Phil, have you ever had a funny feeling that something amazing is going to happen to you? I mean, something you've always wanted to happen without knowing that you wanted it, something that'll never let you be the same again?"

"No," said Phil.

"Neither have I," I said. "Sad, isn't it?"

Someone had thrown up in grand manner outside Fozzer's house, which I didn't think boded particularly well, and there was a young couple inextricably entwined in the hall.

Phil said, "What are they up to?"

I said, "I think it's a tonsillectomy."

We carried our flagons of cider into the kitchen, where we met Garganzo. It was a toss-up whether he was trying to get the contents of a bottle inside himself, or himself inside the bottle. "Great party!" he said. "I'm ratted, mate!"

"Have you been here long?" I said.

"Great party!" said Garganzo. "I'm ratted, mate!"

Phil pinched his nose and said, "I'm sorry, caller, we are unable to connect you with the planet Garganzo at this time." Then he popped a can of lager and took it straight down. I couldn't even see him swallowing.

I said, "Take it easy, Phil."

"Why?"

I couldn't think of a reason, so I decided to join him. I opened a can and drank some, and it made me gag. "This stuff's vile!"

"Of course it is!" said Phil. "You're not supposed to *taste* it! Shall we mingle with the merry throng in the next room?"

The living room was a giant squid—all arms and legs and glistening skin. The music was loud enough to rearrange my internal organs. I'd just adjusted to it when Fozzer appeared and gave me a hearty slap on the back. "Stewart, my dear chap!" he said. "I haven't seen you since the last time I saw you. Enjoying the do?"

I said, "Brilliant, Fozz."

"It is rather splendid, isn't it?" Fozzer said. "You will pardon me, won't you—only I'm in the middle of a fascinating conversation with a couple of identical twins. Either that or I'm having trouble focusing."

He wavered off and I began to say something to Phil, but he was dancing with two girls. I could have joined him, but I suddenly felt that coming to the party had been a bad idea.

And then Lucy was standing in front of me with a

big smile on her face. I had to blink to make sure she was real.

"Hello, Lights!" she said.

I said, "Hello, Dance."

"I wasn't expecting to see you!" Lucy said, and she sounded really pleased.

"I came on impulse," I said. "I'm not really a party person."

Lucy put her head on one side in a way that reminded me of a curious robin eyeing a bread crumb. "Why not?"

"Oh, you know—all the people."

"That's the whole point!" said Lucy. "You can lose yourself in people and be who you want. So who do you want to be?"

I started to dissolve in her eyes and all at once there weren't a lot of people at the party, just Lucy. I said, "The tough questions first, eh?"

Lucy laughed and grabbed my arm. "Dance with me."

"What? Right now?"

Lucy tightened her grip and said, "Dance with me," and she sounded really serious about it, like it was some sort of test.

So I danced with her, but I don't know how I managed it because it felt like I didn't exist from the neck down.

Lucy danced like a cat, and an eagle, and a skein of silk fluttering in the breeze. The dance went right down to the ends of her fingers, and when she made her hair whirl I could see that every strand of it was alive.

I danced like a Clydesdale.

I don't know how long we were dancing, but eventually Lucy noticed that I was flagging and grabbed my arm again. I could feel the warmth of her skin through my sleeve. "Come on, Lights," she said. "You look like you could do with a drink."

She dragged me into the kitchen, found a carton of orange juice on the draining board, poured some into a glass and began to sip it.

I said, "Are you driving?"

When she laughed it made me feel good. I felt like I could devote a lot of time to making her laugh.

"No!" she said. "I hate getting drunk. I hate it when I'm out of control. Don't you?"

"I wouldn't know," I said. "I've never seen you out of control."

"Not a pretty sight," said Lucy.

I didn't believe her.

"You're looking at me," Lucy said.

"I'm sorry. D'you mind?"

"No. I'm going to be a professional dancer. That means I'm going to get looked at for a living."

"You can treat me like a rehearsal, then," I said.

Lucy smiled, and then her eyes went somewhere else. I could see stage lights shining in them.

I thought, Now! Ask her now, before somebody comes in and ruins the moment!

I said, "Lucy, would you like—"

I was interrupted by a terrific roar from the living room. People were shouting, "By the light of the fiery moon! By the light of the fiery moon!"

Lucy frowned, gave a puzzled smile and went out into the hallway to look. I followed.

The crowd in the living room had cleared a circle in the center of the room, and in the middle of the circle stood Fozzer and Alby. Alby was holding a bottle of brandy and a cigarette lighter and waving his arms like a conductor while everybody shouted, "By the light of the fiery moon!"

Fozzer dropped his shorts and exposed his bottom. Alby poured brandy over it and lit the brandy with the lighter. As ghostly blue flames played over Fozzer's backside, people began to sing, "By the light of the fiery moon!" and I heard an angry thumping on the wall from the next-door neighbor's house.

I said, "I think this might be a good time to leave," but I was talking to myself, because Lucy wasn't there. I patrolled the house, but she'd vanished so completely that I wondered if I'd dreamt her.

Phil and I left a lot later—about five minutes before the police arrived. Phil was completely gone and kept staggering against me.

"That was the best party!" he said. "The best party I've ever been to. And you're my best mate!"

I said, "I know, Phil. You're my best mate too."

Phil said, "And you know why you're my best mate, mate? Because I've never had a mate who's better than you are! And you know what?"

I said, "What?"

"I'm going to be sick," said Phil.

And he was.

scene III

casey

when i woke up on sunday morning i was two people.
One was streetwise and cynical with a mouth; the other
was a complete wet who memorized the words to love
songs and wondered when they were going to happen
to her. The two people were fighting and I just couldn't
get my head together at all.

My mind played back the Dean tapes. I couldn't remember everything he'd said—just most of it—and I
couldn't remember everything about him, but what I
did remember was how it had felt to be with him. I was

just about to want to feel that way again, when I didn't. I mean, I saw wet thoughts coming and I stomped on them. I remembered Ryan Wallis and how gutted and betrayed I'd been.

I went downstairs to find Dad frying bacon in the kitchen. Sunday mornings are routine in our house— Dad cooks breakfast for himself and Mum and takes it up to their bedroom, and they eat it while they listen to the radio.

I was heavily into my breakfast-is-just-a-cup-of-black-coffee phase, so I gave Dad some face and said, "How can you eat slices of dead animal first thing in the morning?"

Dad said, "With a hefty dollop of Worcester sauce. Have fun last night?"

I suppose he was just trying to have a chat, but this big neon sign in my head started going PRIVACY INVASION!

I said, "Mff."

"Sorry I asked."

I made myself a cup of coffee, grabbed the arts section and went for a sprawl on the sofa in the sitting room. I'd just got comfortable when the phone rang. I went into the hall to answer it and this voice went, "Hello, can I speak to Casey, please?"

"She's speaking," I said.

"Oh, hi!" said the voice. "It's Dean."

I must have been quiet for a long time because Dean

said, "Remember me? I'm the guy who spent ages talking to you in the garden."

"Of course I remember you!" I said. "How did you find out my number?"

"After you left I asked around until I found someone who knew you. D'you mind?"

"Why should I?"

"You know," said Dean, switching to his cold voice, "sometimes you say things at parties and then, the next morning, it doesn't seem such a great idea."

"No, I'm really glad you rang," I said. "I've been thinking about you."

"And I've been thinking about you."

It was my turn to speak, but I didn't know what was supposed to come next.

Dean said, "I'm working tonight, but I'd really like to see you again. Will you meet me this afternoon?"

"Where?"

"You know that park behind the town hall?"

"Yeah."

"Meet you by the benches in that big shelter. Two-thirty. OK?"

I said, "See you there, then."

Dean hung up, but I kept the phone pressed to my ear, listening to the dial tone while I tried to believe what had just happened.

That's when I noticed Dad. He was halfway down

the stairs and he was giving me this funny look. I looked at myself and saw that while I'd been talking to Dean I'd wound the phone cord round my shoulders and lifted one foot off the floor.

Dad said, "Have you joined the Freemasons?"

"Can't I even have a phone call without being spied on?"

"Do you want a hand getting out of that?"

"I can manage! I'm a big girl now. There's no need to fuss over me!"

Dad said, "I was worried about the phone."

I was so excited, I think I may have eaten some spinach with my lunch. I helped Mum and Dad load the dishwasher, and when Al went to watch telly, I said, "I think I might take a walk this afternoon."

"Good idea!" said Dad. "Why don't we all go? We could drive down to Pebbly Beach and walk along the seafront."

I was like, Oh, n-o-o! I don't need this! I said, "I'm meeting someone."

"Who?" said Mum.

"Dean," I said.

"Dean?" said Dad. "What is he, principal of an American high school?"

"Ha, ha. There goes another rib."

"What's Dean like?" Mum said in her scalpel voice.

"*I* think he's nice," I said.

Dad frowned at me. "You only *think* he's nice? Aren't you sure?"

"Not yet. That's why I'm meeting him."

"Fair enough," said Dad. "Don't be late for tea."

The sun came out while I was walking down Newhouse Hill. I could see the sea, and there were cloud shadows moving over it, but the bits in between reflected the sunshine so brightly that it made my eyes ache. The light made everything look new.

Churchill Park is in a dip at the bottom of Newhouse Hill, but the top of the shelter's on St. Mary's Avenue, the road above it. There are these wooden benches where you can sit and look down on the people lawn bowling—if your life is so sad that you haven't got anything better to do, that is.

No bowling matches were on when I arrived. The only person in the park was an old lady taking her Yorkshire terrier for a walk.

It was twenty-five past two. I sat down on a bench and started having doubts. He won't come. He's changed his mind. He gets his kicks out of setting up stupid little schoolgirls and letting them down.

Then I heard this motorbike pull up behind me, and Dean was riding it. He propped up the bike, pulled off his crash helmet so his hair spilled out over his face and walked toward me, smiling.

Sometimes meeting people again is a downer,

because they don't look as good as you remember. I thought maybe my memory of Dean had got mixed up with the starlight, but it hadn't. He looked better than I remembered, and I forgot about being cynical and streetwise. I was in Sappyville, heading straight for the city center.

Dean sat down next to me and said, "I'm glad you're here."

"So am I. If I wasn't, you'd be talking to yourself and people would think you were a complete weirdo."

Dean laughed and spun his helmet between his hands. "I enjoyed talking last night," he said. "Most people . . ."

"What?"

"Talking's not easy, you know?" said Dean. "People aren't that interested in the things I want to talk about. You're different."

"That's me—Casey the freak!" I said.

"No, I mean, usually when I talk to girls at parties I don't remember them afterward, but I remembered you. It feels like you and I really met last night."

"I bet you say that to all the girls," I said. Dumb, right? I sounded like my gran or something. I started to blush, but then Dean made it OK by looking me straight in the eyes and saying, "No, I don't."

"I'm sorry," I said. "I'm not very good at this."

"Tell me about it! I've never done this before."

"What, you've never talked to a girl before?"

"Not like this," said Dean. "In Spain, when I was wound up, I used to go to this little bay where no one else went. I'd sit on a rock and watch the waves come in until I felt better. Talking to you makes me feel like that. I think I could tell you anything."

Know what to say when someone tells you something like that? Nothing. If you say anything, it'll come out sounding pathetic.

We talked. I found out Dean was a trainee chef at Merry Munchas, this place on the divided highway just outside town. It was a crap job, but he needed the money, and so did his family.

"Other nineteen-year-olds are raking it in," said Dean. "But there you go, it's all I could get."

I was like, DEAN IS NINETEEN! REPEAT, DEAN IS NINETEEN! *START PANICKING!*

"What do you do?" said Dean.

I said, "I'm still in school."

"Applying to universities."

This is when I could have told him the truth, but I figured if he found out I wasn't sixteen yet it would put him off. Something was happening between us, but it was as fragile as a soap bubble and I didn't want it to pop.

"My parents want me to," I said—which was true, but I left out the part about finishing high school first.

"D'you always do what your parents want?" said Dean. "Haven't you got a mind of your own?"

"Sure—but they pay the bills."

Dean told me some more about himself, and I told him more about me, and somewhere in the conversation it became OK to laugh. We laughed a lot, and all of a sudden it wasn't a conversation, it was a stroll through each other. It was so totally amazing that I forgot to listen to what we were saying.

I remember one thing, though. We were talking about things we were afraid of and Dean said, "People are my phobia."

I remember, because that's the moment I decided to take Dean on. I could see there was hurt in him and I thought I could make it better. I thought I could take his fear away and get him to trust.

The town hall clock struck four. Dean pulled a face and said, "I'd better get back and get ready for work."

"A chef's gotta do what a chef's gotta do!" I said.

"I'll see you again."

"When?"

"I'll give you a call." He got on the motorbike and started tucking his hair inside his helmet. "Which way you walking?" he said.

I pointed up Newhouse Hill.

"I'll go the other way, then," said Dean. "You go first, and don't turn round."

"Why not?"

"When you leave someone, you shouldn't look back."

So I walked away and I didn't look back, not even when I heard him start up the motorbike. I kept my eyes looking straight ahead, and I knew that something had happened to me.

I was wonderful.

scene IV

on sunday morning I woke up feeling like a crypt, and everybody buried in it had died young. My life was a disaster. I was only good at things I didn't care about, like getting good grades. Otherwise I was always saying the wrong things to the wrong people at the wrong times, or even worse, not saying anything at all.

I could see what was going to happen with Lucy: I was going to chicken out, and she'd end up with some thick, handsome hulk who wouldn't appreciate her.

I thought, That's what always happens. The girls I fall in love with always end up with blokes I can't stand.

Then I sat up in bed with goose bumps all over me. I thought, Oh, no! So I *am* in love with Lucy! I just admitted it!

I told myself that it wasn't going to do any good to lie in bed wallowing in self-pity; mind you, it wasn't going to do me any good if I didn't, but if I got up at least I'd feel like I was making some sort of effort.

My parents were in the kitchen. Mum was joining in with Singing Christians on the radio and Dad was humming to himself.

"You two are cheerful this morning," I said. "Did we win the lottery?"

Mum gave me one of her how-could-you-possibly-have-forgotten looks and said, "Frank's coming home today."

"Oh, right," I said.

"Well, you might sound a little more enthusiastic about it!" said Dad.

The trouble was, I didn't feel enthusiastic. Frank had just finished his first term at university and I'd got used to his not being around. Now I was going to have to spend Christmas with him.

It's not that I don't like Frank—he's so charming it's impossible not to like him—it's just that, where I am a crypt, Frank's a marble ballroom with crystal chandeliers.

"I'm so overwhelmed I can hardly speak," I told Dad.

"Sarcasm!" he said. "The lowest form of wit."

Dad has a lot of little sayings like that; I think he had to learn them for his prep-school entrance exams.

"The train's due in at twelve-thirty," said Mum. "I think we should all go and meet him."

I said, "What, me as well?"

"Of course you as well!" said Mum. "It's the longest Frank's ever been away from home. We've got to make him feel welcome, haven't we?"

If I'd been in a sassier mood I would have suggested lying down in muddy pools so that Frank could walk over us, but I didn't, because Mum and Dad would have accused me of jealousy.

And I was jealous. I suppose my parents must have talked about me sometimes, but I only noticed when they talked about Frank. Mum had got into the habit of going misty-eyed every now and again and saying, "I wonder what Frank's doing now?"

"He'll expect his own brother to be there," said Dad.

This meant that Dad expected me to be there. The thought of being one big, happy family again plunged me into deep gloom.

Frank's train was early, so by the time we got down to the station he was already outside waiting for us. If I have to wait for anybody I go hunched and jittery, but Frank waits really well. He is tall and firm and confident-looking. When he noticed the car his smile was dazzling.

We piled out to greet him. Frank hugged Mum, went, "Whoo!" like Americans do instead of laughing, picked her up off her feet and swung her round.

I wanted to shrivel up and die.

"Hey, bro!" Frank gave me a mock punch on the shoulder.

I said, "Hey, bro!" and punched him back.

There was a lot of chatter in the car—none of it mine—and then Mum said, "We bought a lovely Christmas tree yesterday, Frank. You and Stewart can put the decorations on later, like you always do."

"Great!" said Frank.

I thought, *Groan!*

Ideally, I would have draped the tree with black ribbons and put my bleeding heart on top of it, but, instead, I had to drag out all the battered shoe boxes of decorations from the cupboard under the stairs. As we unpacked them, Frank said, "This fairy looks a bit miserable, doesn't she?"

"How would you look if you knew someone was going to shove a Christmas tree up your dress?" I said.

I don't know how many times I'd put that fairy on top of a Christmas tree—I can remember having to be lifted up to do it when I was very young—but this time I noticed that she wasn't a fairy at all. She was a cardboard ballerina in a white net dress, with yellow hair and faded blue eyes. She made me think of Lucy. I remembered dancing at the party and the warmth of Lucy's hand on my arm.

"How's your love life?" said Frank.

"Not," I said. "How's yours?"

"Kicking," said Frank.

I looked round the tree to see if he was joking. "Really?"

"I'm deeply smitten," Frank said. "Or is it smighted?"

"It's smought," I said. "Who is she?"

Frank's reply lasted all the way through untangling tinsel. She was Francesca. She was a law student and she was completely wonderful. Her hair, her voice, her laugh—even her eyelashes—were wonderful. Frank told me some of her side-splittingly witty remarks, but I guessed you had to have been there at the time to appreciate them.

Frank said, "And when she wakes up in the morning, she . . ."

"Hang on!" I said. "How do you know what she does when she wakes up?"

"How d'you think?"

I found the idea a little difficult to handle. This was

Frank, my perfect brother who'd never done anything wrong. Intellectual-giant Frank, who had also managed to win the school champion medal three sports days in a row. I didn't know he'd had time for anything else. There had always been girls around Frank, but he'd never gone in for anything serious.

Frank started laughing. "Your face!" he said. "You look like a vicar who's just farted in Harrods!"

"I always thought you were just a big brain."

"I spent high school working hard and being good," said Frank. "When I hit university I decided that I deserved a wild time." Then his face went serious. "Er, don't tell Mum and Dad, will you? I mean, I am working, only . . ."

I said, "Don't worry, Frank. I won't let on that you're normal."

It was all right after that. Over dinner, while he was talking about his courses, Frank kept giving me a look like we were in on something together.

On Monday Frank and I went into town. He wanted to buy Christmas presents, and I went with him because I wanted to find out more about the person he'd turned into. There seemed to be a distinct danger of our getting along.

We went into Owen's. Frank bought Mum something scenty and Dad something practical. On the way out he said, "I'm starving. Fancy a burger?"

"I thought you were a penniless student?" I said.

Frank said, "Who said I was going to pay?"

We went to Burger King. It was packed. The only seats were right in the front window. I wasn't too happy because I felt so exposed, like a zoo specimen, but Frank wasn't fazed at all. He spread himself out until he filled his half of the booth. "This is weird!" he said. "Why is town so different when it's the same?"

"Because you've changed," I said.

Frank's face went thoughtful. I could tell I was right, and he was impressed.

Someone tapped on the outside of the window and I jumped about three feet. It was Lucy. She was wearing a dark blue overcoat and a big smile. Her hair was pinned up and wisps of it were trailing over her face. She put her head on one side, held up her hand and wiggled her fingers in a wave.

I didn't just melt, I vaporized. I waved back. Lucy's smile went up to ten on the Richter scale; then she twirled round and was gone.

"Who was *that*?" said Frank.

"Er, Lucy," I said.

"Is she your girlfriend?"

"I wish!"

"Have you been out with her?"

"No."

"Why not?"

"Well . . . you know. I'd like to, but I sort of haven't got round to asking her yet."

Frank stared at me as though I were an alien life-form. He said, "You mean a girl who looks like she does smiles at you the way she just did . . . and you haven't asked her out yet?"

"Well . . . you know," I said.

"Yes, I do," said Frank. "Come on." He grabbed me by the shoulders and hauled me to my feet.

"Where are we going? I haven't finished my burger!"

"There's more to life than half-eaten cheeseburgers."

He manhandled me onto the street. It was packed with shoppers. Frank looked around, then pointed and said, "There she is!"

I was horribly certain about what was going to happen next, but I couldn't stop it. Frank's hand went up to his mouth, he cupped his fingers and shouted, "Hey, Lucy!"

I think it was the loudest sound I'd ever heard. Hundreds of faces turned to stare and I wished I could be somewhere else. One of the faces was Lucy's. She noticed Frank and looked puzzled; then she noticed me and looked pleased.

"Wait a minute!" Frank yelled. "Stewart wants to ask you something!" Then he gave me a shove and said, "Go for it!"

I thought, Earth, swallow me! Sky, fall on my head!

I reached Lucy, but when I tried to think of something to say my tongue was blank.

"Hello, Lights!" said Lucy.

"Hello, Dance," I said.

"Who's that?" said Lucy, looking at Frank.

"My big brother," I said. "Loud, isn't he?"

Lucy said, "I'm really sorry about the other night. I didn't notice how late it was, and when I did I panicked and . . ."

"It doesn't matter," I said, then seized up. High Street wasn't the right place to talk to Lucy, and I had to get away somehow.

"Did you really want to ask me something?" Lucy said.

I was going to make it into a joke and say that Frank was just trying to embarrass me, but instead I said, "Would you like to go out with me?"

Lucy said, "Uh-huh."

I said, "Sorry? Was that uh-huh, yes, or uh-huh, push off?"

Lucy laughed. "You're crazy!" she said. "Of course I'd like to go out with you. Give me a call and we'll fix something up."

"I don't know your number," I said.

"We're the last Dixon in the book," said Lucy. "Must rush now—and call me, right?"

"Right!"

She disappeared into the crowd and I stood there like the brainless idiot I felt.

Frank came over. "She said yes, didn't she?" he said.

I said, "Hmm!"

"I knew she would!"

"Hmm!"

"Just tell me one thing, will you?" said Frank.

"What?"

"What have you got that I haven't got?"

scene V

Did I think about Dean, or what? I thought about him so much, I was afraid he'd wear out. I couldn't get him out of my head any more than you can cure yourself of the flu. I had Dean like an illness and I didn't want to get better.

You know those merry-go-rounds they have at fairgrounds—the ones for the toddlers? They've got little pink horses, and fire engines, and dinky planes, and they go round really, really slowly. Well, until now, my life had been stuck on one of those. I'd been on a pink horse, going round with nice, safe people my parents approved of, and I wanted off.

Dean was something else. Dean was a ticket for the log ride. He was upfront, not quite respectable, and dangerous. Dean was someone my parents definitely wouldn't approve of, which was part of his appeal, because I'd had it with being a good girl. I wanted to go tap-dancing with tigers.

I didn't think I was in love yet, but I was falling in love. For the first time I understood why it was called 'falling,' because I had no more control over myself than if I'd tripped. And I was enjoying it—the aching to see Dean, the excitement, the scary feeling. I got up on Monday morning feeling that I'd explode if I didn't talk to someone about it.

Mum and Dad had left for work, but Al was around. He was making himself a potato chip and chutney sandwich in the kitchen. I was in a brilliant mood so I decided to spread it around and treat him like a human being. I said, "Hey, Al! How're things?"

Al said, "No."

I said, "Huh?"

"Whatever you're after, the answer's no."

"I'm not after anything."

"Then it must be a scam and I'm not falling for it."

"This is nice!" I said. "This is a caring, sharing family."

Al said, "Bog off!"

I rang Helen and we arranged to meet in town. There was some stuff I wanted to get, like wrapping paper and Al's present. I'd decided to buy him a CD of Occasional Duck, this band he was into.

Town was hell. It was heaving with people doing last-minute shopping. Someone had rigged up speakers on the streetlamps and they were belting out, "'Tis the season to be jolly, fa-la-la-la-la . . . !" but the shoppers weren't having any of it.

Helen met me on the square outside the town hall. As soon as I saw her I knew something was up, because she had her secretive face on. I was busting to get going on Dean, but Helen stopped me by saying, "This boy fancies me."

"What boy?" I said.

"I don't know."

I adjusted my translation unit to Helenese and tried again. "Which boy you don't know?"

"I can't remember!" said Helen. "It was someone who danced with me at Fozzer's party. Tina rang me up yesterday and said that this boy had been asking about me."

She was really psyched up. I said, "Take it easy. Whatever's going to happen, will happen." I know it didn't mean anything, but it was the sort of thing you said to Helen when she was in frightened-rabbit mode.

It worked. Helen smiled and said, "Tina told me a boy was asking about you after we left on Saturday."

"I know," I said. "He found me."

I went into detail about Dean. I talked all the way through buying Al's CD in HMV, and all the way through buying wrapping paper in the art shop. I'd been expecting Helen to be pleased, but when I finished telling her she went, "Oh, dear!"

"Oh, dear, what?"

"He's nineteen."

"It's OK, Hel," I said. "I'm into older men."

"But if he's as gorgeous as you say, why hasn't he got a girlfriend his own age?"

I said, "He thinks he has."

Helen frowned; then her face relaxed as she worked it out. "You mean you haven't told him how old you are? Oh, dear!"

"What's the big deal?" I said. "I'm sixteen soon, then Dean will only be three years older than I am. So what? When he's a hundred, I'll be ninety-seven, what difference does it make?"

Helen gave me this look like she knew exactly what difference it made but she wasn't saying. She said, "I hope it works out."

"Of course it'll work out! It's not like I want to have a heavy relationship or anything."

Helen does a really good unconvinced look, and she

did one then. I was just about to have a go at her for it when something dead weird happened.

These two guys came bursting out of Burger King and one of them started shouting, right in the middle of High Street. At first I thought he was mentally challenged, or high, but then I saw him shove the other guy toward a girl who was standing staring at him.

"Isn't that Lucy Dixon?" said Helen.

"I think so," I said.

"I wonder what's going on? I thought she was so dedicated to dancing that she didn't have anything to do with boys," Helen said.

I watched. The guy talking to Lucy was really nervous and he was standing like he was afraid to move in case he broke.

I thought, This is where old Lucy Iron-drawers smashes him and leaves him in pieces on the pavement!

But then Lucy nodded at something the guy said and gave him a yummy smile. It was the biggest smile I'd ever seen her give to an audience of one.

"It's love," I said.

"You reckon?" said Helen.

"Definitely. It's getting very popular, you know."

"You can't really blame her," said Helen.

"Why not?"

"He's a bit dishy, isn't he?"

"I suppose so," I said. "If you go for that type."

Helen gave me a look and said, "You *have* got it bad, haven't you?" Then she sighed. "I wish the boy I can't remember would ring me up so I could find out who he was. Then I'd know whether I wanted him to ring me up or not."

Mum and Dad were in when I got home. They were on the sofa in the sitting room watching the news. I flashed my look-at-me-I'm-terrific smile, and Mum said, "What's wrong?"

"Nothing," I said.

"Then why are you smiling?" said Mum. She looked down to check her clothes. "Do I look funny or something?"

I said, "No! Look, I was just smiling, OK?"

"Casey," said Mum, "I've known you for the last fifteen years and you don't just smile. Are you in trouble?"

"No, I'm happy."

"Don't worry," said Dad, "it'll soon pass."

"Great! If I'm happy, it makes my mother paranoid and my father cynical! Thanks a lot for your understanding and support!"

"Wouldn't it be nice if we could get through just one day without a disagreement?" Dad said.

I said, "What disagreement? Who's disagreeing? I haven't disagreed with anything! How comes it's all my fault?"

I didn't get it. I mean, I knew my parents had been my age once because I'd seen photos of them. Mum had talked to me about her old boyfriends and how difficult it was for her and Dad to get together when his parents didn't approve of her, but it was like she remembered what happened and forgot how it felt.

When I was up about something I was intense. I fizzed like a firework just before it goes off, and everything was sparks, light and music. When I was down, the world was a black pit with no yesterday, today or tomorrow.

My parents must have been like that once, but now everything has flattened out so there are no highs or lows, and they act like that is the only way to be.

I hoped Dean would call. All evening, I perched on the edge of my chair so I could rush out and grab the phone as soon as it rang and be the first person to hear his voice. The hope started out bright, but as it got later and later it tarnished and wore down into depression.

I needed therapy, so I went to make some hot chocolate. If you've ever considered getting soulful while you're waiting for a kettle to boil, I'm here to tell you it can't be done.

Dad came into the kitchen and made out like he hadn't followed me deliberately, but I could tell. "Oh, there you are!" he said, trying to sound surprised.

"I can't help it. I live here."

"So do I," said Dad. "You should try talking to me sometime."

"Why?"

"I might be able to give you some wise advice."

"If I paid any attention to wise advice, being young would be a waste of time, wouldn't it?"

Dad's eyes went between angry and hurt. It made me want to hug him, but I didn't because I figured he was doing it deliberately, and I wasn't going to be emotionally blackmailed.

"I do worry about you, you know," Dad said.

"It'll soon pass," I said. "It's probably just a phase you're going through."

scene VI

stew

Mr. Hart had been right—asking Lucy out had been that easy after all. The only real difficulty had been me, and I'd cracked it. I wanted to call her as soon as I got in on Monday afternoon, but then I started thinking. If I rushed it, I'd come over as being neurotic; leaving it until Tuesday would seem more laid-back and mature. Also, I had some problems to confront.

First problem was the phone. I'm useless on the phone; I've never been able to actually believe that there's a real person on the other end. As soon as I pick one up, what I mean to say evaporates down the fiber-optic cable and I either chatter about anything that comes into my head, or I just say "Hmm" and "No." Not a lot to choose between Mr. Airhead and Mr. Sulky, is there?

I'm good at conversations in books. Stick a bit of dialogue from a novel or a play in front of me and I can analyze it like anything. I'll dissect it and wrap it up with a bow on top. Real conversations are trickier, because it's more difficult to work out why people are saying things.

The second problem was where to go on a date. When it came to a romantic setting where a young couple could have an intimate tête-à-tête, I didn't have many choices. The movies was the best bet, but the only thing worth seeing was the latest Disney cartoon, and it didn't exactly go with laid-back and mature.

I was pondering all this when Phil rang. He sounded terrible, even for Phil.

"What's with you?" I said.

Phil said, "I need to talk. Not on the phone, this is a pub job."

"OK."

"Meet you in the Northgate at seven-thirty," said Phil.

"Phil, no one goes to the Northgate!"

"Precisely."

The Northgate wasn't so much downbeat as primitive.

It was at the seedy end of town, near what was left of the docks. Once it had been a notorious pub, full of sailors who wanted to drink, fight and get laid, and though the sailors were long gone, the Northgate's reputation clung on.

On the way there I was nervous about going in, but when I arrived it was sad. An old couple was sitting at a table in one corner, staring at nothing. I got the strange feeling that they'd always been there, and if I went closer I'd see a thick layer of dust floating on the surface of their drinks.

Phil was in another corner, also staring at nothing.

The barmaid looked extremely tired, and when I asked for a half-pint of bitter she said, "Is that beer?"

I said, "Er, yes, it is."

I sat at Phil's table and smiled at him, but the smile went straight into his face and never came back. I said, "Phil, are you feeling a bit down?"

"I've done something incredibly stupid."

From the tone of his voice, I thought it must be drugs—or AIDS at least. "What is it, mate?" I said.

"The only thing I can remember about Fozzer's party is this girl I danced with," said Phil. "I woke up thinking about her on Sunday morning and I tried to stop but . . ." Phil shrugged and took a pull at his pint. I sipped my half and immediately wished I hadn't. "I'm obsessed," said Phil.

I said, "Steady! Just remember that it's quite normal."

"Not for me it isn't!" said Phil. "I don't get daffy over girls—that's your department!" He took a piece of paper from his pocket, unfolded it and smoothed it out on the table so I could see what was written on it. "I practically begged to get that," he said.

"It's a phone number, isn't it?"

"*Her* phone number," Phil said. "I don't know what to do with it."

"Er, phone her?"

"I've tried. When I get to the phone, my heart starts thumping, my mouth goes dry and my palms sweat. D'you think I'm sick or something?"

"No," I said. "I think you've got 'it.'"

Phil went pale. "It isn't what I think it is, is it? One word, four letters, first letter *L*?"

"Sounds like it to me," I said.

"I was afraid of that. That's why I wanted to talk to you here. I didn't want anyone else to know."

As far as the rest of our class was concerned, Phil was Iron Man—the bloke without sentiment who laughed at romantic films and said that football was more interesting than sex. He had a reputation to protect.

Phil said, "I don't understand this at all. I don't even believe it exists! It's just a self-induced delusion with its roots in the urge to procreate."

I said, "But if it doesn't exist, how come you're in it?"

"I haven't told you the worst part," said Phil. He leant across the table and whispered, "She's a freshman."

"Oh?"

"I mean, it's pathetic for someone my age to be eating his heart out over a ninth-grade girl!"

"Girls mature faster than boys," I said. "Remember Romeo and Juliet? She was only thirteen."

"I know," said Phil, "and look what happened to them! What am I going to do?"

"Call her," I said.

"There must be something else I can try!" He sank his pint and looked at the glass. "I think I need another."

"You won't find the answer in a glass."

"I know," said Phil, "but it's a good way of forgetting the question."

In the end, Phil didn't have another drink. We went for a walk and he talked, and it was like listening to myself.

It was a cold, clear night—good for talking. The sidewalks were damp and there was a haze round the streetlights. We walked up to Seaview Terrace, where the houses were boarded up, and looked out over the ruined docks. The moon shone on piles of rusty iron.

"I used to be so in control!" groaned Phil. "Now I'm losing myself! Is it always so scary?"

I said, "It's delicious agony, Phil. The part that's hardest to get used to is that you never get used to it."

"It was just me on my own," said Phil. "I wasn't bothered about letting anyone else into my life. Now it's . . ."

"I know," I said.

"So," said Phil, "you think I should use that number, then?"

"Do it!"

"Right."

I left him at the corner of Hotchkiss Street, and it felt like I was bidding farewell to a condemned man.

On the way home I saw a couple kissing in the shadows under a lime tree. They were so lost in one another that they didn't notice me. I thought, There's a lot of it about, and the thought grew.

Act III scene I

Dean finally rang me on Tuesday, the day before christmas eve. He called from work, and there was a lot of clanking and shouting in the background. He said, "Sorry I haven't rung before, I've been real busy." I said, "That's fine!", which it hadn't been.

"I'm working tomorrow, and then I'm tied up with the family," said Dean, "but I could meet you Saturday if you like."

"I like," I said.

Dean said, "Same time, same place?"

I said, "Sure."

There was a pause. I could hear Dean's breath sounding like breaking waves. Just before he hung up, he said, "I wish I could see your eyes." He said it really quickly and put the phone down straightaway so I wouldn't have a chance to say anything.

Time went gray. You know how as you get older time seems to speed up? Well, I regressed to about four, and the three days I had to wait felt like forever.

I've hated Christmas since I was twelve. I'm always stuck with my family when I'd rather be doing things with other people somewhere else. And my parents act as if Al and I still get a kick out of doing things we used to enjoy when we were little. We have to get up on Christmas morning and go through the presents ritual—round the tree in the sitting room, taking it in turns to open our parcels—then comes the Christmas lunch ritual. We pull crackers, put on stupid paper hats, watch the Queen's Speech, and then Dad drinks two glasses of port and falls asleep in front of the big film, just the same as the year before. . . .

One weird thing this year, though: When I pulled my cracker there was a little plastic motorbike inside. It was green, and there was a key ring on a chain stuck in it. I was like, DEAN SYMBOL! A MESSAGE FROM DESTINY! until it turned out that all the crackers had plastic motorbike key rings in them, so it looked like

Destiny's message was "There's nothing special about you, kid!"

The day after Christmas was leftover turkey and the ritual visit to Gran. I kept looking at my watch and thinking, Come on, will you? Go faster so I can get to *my* day! It was like having to eat a piece of bread and butter before I was allowed to get at the cream cakes.

I came out of the gray at twenty past two the next day, as I was walking down Newhouse Hill. I got spooked. I'd been waiting for so long, I'd forgotten how to do anything else. What if it didn't go right? What if Dean had changed his mind about me? What if it turned out that what we had could get lost as easily as we'd found it?

Dean was waiting for me. His bike was parked at the side of the road next to the shelter, and he was leaning against it with his hands in his pockets. I ran toward him, because if it was all fouled up I wanted to know quickly. When I reached him, I was so out of breath that I couldn't say anything.

Dean didn't move or smile, he just looked at me. In cheesy romance books they put stuff like "their eyes met," but it wasn't like that. Dean's eyes hoovered me up and my brain started dancing in the tiger's cage.

"You're taller than I remembered," said Dean.

"I'm a growing girl," I said. "Is it a problem?"

"No," said Dean. "But have you noticed how people change size when you get to know them better?"

"D'you know me better?"

"Maybe," said Dean. He reached down to the bike and held out a helmet. "Ever ridden a motorbike before?"

"Where are we going?"

"Where would you like to go?"

"Wherever you want to take me." I thought, Well, get a load of Miss Nonchalant!

Actually, I was terrified. All I knew about motorbikes was TEENS MANGLED IN MOTORBIKE MAYHEM, but I tried to act cool.

Dean helped me with the helmet and showed me where to put my feet when I sat down. "You'll have to put your arms round my waist and hold on tight," he said.

"I think I can hack that bit," I said.

When you're in a car, you're in a cozy metal box that stays still while everything else moves. On a bike, you can see the road underneath and the white lines flicking like strobe lights. The air blew inside my jacket and gave me bodybuilder's shoulders. I heard heavy metal guitars in my head, and it was me. I was Rebel Girl, roaring off on the back of a bike with my middle finger stuck up at everything.

That was for the first two hundred yards. Dean

must have been doing eight miles an hour, and I was crazed with speed.

We went through town, and then Dean hung a left at All Hallows church and we went down the hill into Corncroft Woods. Shadows of trees flashed across my face, and it was like we were flying through a zebra.

We stopped in a carpark next to a pitch-and-putt green. Dean chained up the bike and the helmets, and we followed a path that went over a bridge and ended in a high bank of pebbles. From the top of the bank there was a view of the sea.

"I like this place," Dean said.

I'd been there loads of times, because Pebbly Beach was where all the locals went while the day-trippers packed themselves onto the sand in the next bay down. With Dean it was like I'd never been there before. The wind tasted salty, and there was that knocking sound pebbles make when the waves drag them backward. You could see them in the foam, like jumping bread rolls.

I said, "Yeah, it's pretty, isn't it?" This is probably the most idiotic thing I've ever said to anyone, but Dean acted like he hadn't heard me. "Was that bay in Spain like this?" I said.

"No," said Dean. "You weren't there." Then he looked at me, dead serious, and said, "Are you any good at skimming?"

"At *what*?"

"Skimming. You know, bouncing pebbles on the water."

"I haven't thought about it a lot," I said.

"Let's find out, then."

He grabbed my hand, and a shock went across my shoulders and down to the backs of my knees—and then we were running down the pebbly bank toward the sea, and I was laughing like a maniac.

We goofed around like a pair of kids. Dean picked up some flat pebbles. I found a rude-shaped one and giggled at it. Dean took a pebble, weighed it in his hand and said, "This is me." He flicked his wrist as he threw the pebble, and it went skimming over the water. It bounced five times before it sank.

I said, "And this is me."

My pebble went straight up, and straight down— *kaplonk!*

"There you go," I said. "You're a bouncer and I'm a plonker."

We threw more stones and had more laughs. Dean said he'd show me how to skim, but when he held my hand it suddenly wasn't about throwing stones anymore. He put both his hands round mine and turned my hand over so he could look at my palm. "You've got nice fingers," he said.

"I didn't mean to," I said. "I was born with them."

"Where'd you get that scar?"

"Elementary school. I was mucking round with a desk lid and my finger got stuck in the hinge."

"You're cold," said Dean. "Let's get out of the wind."

We found a hollow in the pebbles that someone must have used as a suntrap the summer before. I lay down in it and looked at the sky. Dean sat near me. His hair was blowing all over the place and he had to keep pulling it out of his eyes.

"Why don't you come down here?" I said.

We lay on our sides, facing each other. Dean said, "Have you been here before with anyone?"

"No," I said.

All the quiet in the world dropped onto us and something I couldn't stop moved my head toward Dean's and we kissed. It was an A+ kiss. His lips weren't slobbery or flaky, just soft and warm, with the warm going right down inside me. We didn't bang noses or click teeth, the way you do when a first kiss is awkward. This kiss had been waiting for a long time and it didn't do anything to blow its chances.

We came out of it and Dean said, "That was really good."

"You should have been on my end of it," I said, "it was terrific!"

Dean frowned and sat up again. His hair went wild in the wind.

"What's up?" I said. "Are you sorry you kissed me?"

"No, but I ought to be."

I thought, Thirty seconds ago I was snogging this guy, what's going on now?

Dean said, "Talking's all right, but kissing's . . . like caring."

"Is it?" I said.

"It is with you."

"So what's wrong with caring?"

Dean laughed and shook his head, and I thought he was doing it to cover up a hurt place.

I said, "If it's painful, maybe you should stop doing it."

"What?" said Dean.

"Whatever it is you're doing. Come here."

More kissing. If I opened my eyes, I could see the side of Dean's face and the sky; when I closed them, there was nothing else in the world except the two of us. Then things started getting urgent. I felt Dean's hands pulling at the buckle of my belt.

"What are you doing?" I said.

"What d'you think?"

"I'm not sure I want this."

"Come on!" said Dean. "Don't get me all worked up and then let me down."

Pebbles clattered. Dean and I sat up, and there was

a guy standing in front of us. He had gray hair and his face looked really surprised. He must have been walking across the pebbles and nearly trodden on us. "I do beg your pardon!" he said.

Dean was like a dog who'd just seen another dog he didn't like. He started to stand up, but I grabbed his jacket and pulled. I said, "Forget it, Dean."

"I'm going to stick it to him!"

"Leave it! It's all right."

The guy hurried away, but Dean was still tensed up. I could feel him shaking. "People always spoil things!"

"It's all right. Nothing's spoilt."

"How would you know?" said Dean. "What do you know about it, anyway?"

I knelt in front of him. A pebble was sticking in my kneecap, but I ignored it. I held Dean's face in my hands and kissed him. First it was just me doing it, but then he joined in and we were close again. After the kiss, I held him tight and put my head on his shoulder.

Dean said, "We should never have started this."

"Why not?"

"You're nice."

"Well, now you're just being insulting." The joke snapped on him like a piece of raw spaghetti.

"What is this?" he said. "What's going on with you?"

I leaned back to look in his eyes and said, "Why don't we just relax and see where it takes us?"

Dean shook his head, and all the tightness went out of him. His shoulders sagged. "That's fine with me," he said.

The light was going. We knew it was time to go, so we stood up, dusted ourselves off and walked back to the bike. We'd arrived at Pebbly Beach like two kids who wanted to play; but things had got a whole lot more complicated.

•• • •• • •• • •• • •• • •• • •• • •• •

Dean drove me back to Churchill Park and left me there. I was dying to ask him when we were going to meet again, but I didn't want to seem pushy. I could tell he wasn't ready to admit that what we had was special. Maybe he didn't even know it yet, but I did.

Dean rode off. I had a lot of feelings I couldn't name, but I was certain of one thing—I'd just had the best day of my life.

scene II

stew

As soon as the phone rang, someone picked it up and I heard Lucy say, "Hello?"

"Hello, Dance," I said.

I could hear the smile in her voice as she said, "D'you realize I've been hanging around all morning waiting for you to call?"

"I'm sorry," I said, which was a total lie because I was pleased.

Then we both said, "So where shall we . . . ?" and laughed.

"I really want to see the new Disney film," said Lucy. "Will you take me?"

I said, "Tonight?"

"I can't tonight. I've got a dance class."

"You're a bit dedicated, aren't you?"

"Totally," said Lucy. "How about tomorrow night?"

"Christmas Eve?"

"Oh, no! I forgot! What about Saturday?"

"Great!"

"Meet me in the square at six," Lucy said.

"I'll be there."

When I put the phone down, I had an incredible adrenaline rush. I wanted to punch the air and shout, "Yes!" but I restrained myself because Frank was leaning in the living room doorway, giving me moral support.

"Well?" said Frank.

"We have contact!" I said, and then the adrenaline wore off. "What am I going to do?" I said. "What am I going to say?"

"Be yourself," said Frank. "That's who she's interested in."

"How d'you know that?"

Frank came over, put his hand on my shoulder and said, "Be yourself."

I thought, Which one? English Literature Whiz Kid? Matey Twelfth-Grade Bloke? Gibbering Romantic Idiot?

There was more to being myself than Frank realized.

Christmas was low-key, as usual. Mum and Dad went to midnight mass on Christmas Eve and Frank and I waited up until they got back. We opened our presents and finally rolled into bed about two o'clock.

When I was a little kid I used to take my favorite present to bed with me and put it somewhere I could see it as soon as I opened my eyes in the morning. Then, when I'd woken up, I'd lie in bed for ages, looking at it. That's what I did with the thought of Lucy on Christmas morning. I thought if I tried hard enough, I'd be able to get inside her head and find out what she was thinking. I nearly made it too. I could hear the tearing of wrapping paper and the tinkling of angel chimes, and then it turned into a doze that lasted until Frank appeared at the door and told me to haul ass.

On Friday afternoon I went for a long walk to kill time. I followed Harbor Lane all the way down to Pebbly Beach. I'd always wanted to go to Pebbly Beach with someone special. In fact, I used to imagine that if I got up early in the morning and went to Pebbly Beach, I'd find my special someone walking along the seafront, looking for me. But she was never there.

I walked down to the shoreline. The tide was out far enough for stretches of sand to show. The sand was wet, and when I stepped on it the weight of my feet pushed the water out and made pale circles, like white shadows.

The wind was freezing cold, but I didn't mind. I listened to the waves breaking and picked up a small pebble to see how far I could throw it. When I looked I saw it was one of the fossilized shells Dad calls Devil's Toenails. They're quite common, but that afternoon finding one felt important. I closed my fingers round the stone until it went warm, and I thought, This is for Lucy! Then I slipped it into my pocket and forgot about it.

Next evening, I got to the town hall square fifteen minutes early. I can be patient, but if I'm really looking forward to something my patience runs out about an hour before it should; then I've got to make a move.

The big Christmas tree in the middle of the square was all lit up, and the PA system was still churning out Christmas carols. The tape must have stretched because the music kept altering speed and it made the choir sound as though it was singing underwater.

I thought I might look a bit suspicious standing there, so I took a stroll round the tree. You can do a lot of strolling in fifteen minutes.

Just after six, a double-decker pulled up at the bus stop near the phone boxes and Lucy stepped off. She looked around, spotted me and came running over.

"I was really worried you wouldn't be here," she said, and twirled round.

I said, "D'you always dance when you're happy?"

"Yes," said Lucy, "and when I'm sad and when I'm in between. I can't hear a piece of music without choreographing it. I want to turn everything into a dance."

The inside of my head was dancing too, but it had nothing to do with music. I said, "I was afraid of asking you out."

"What?"

"I didn't want you to say no."

Lucy slipped her arm through mine and tugged me until our shoulders bumped together. "You're a madman!" she said.

We walked down High Street. I wanted there to be more people so they could see us together.

"I hoped you'd ask me out," said Lucy. "I would have asked you, but . . ."

"But what?" I said.

"Oh, you know. You Big Senior me Little Freshman."

I said, "Maybe I should have worn my teddy bear suit," and Lucy stuck out her tongue.

The film turned out to be not such a good idea, because Screen One was packed out with kids who had the concentration span of goldfish. They chattered, bounced up and down and laughed too loudly at the jokes.

I was really aware of Lucy's hand on the arm of the

seat next to me. I was trying to edge my hand closer to it so that we'd touch accidentally, when something dramatic happened in the film. The kids all went "Oooh!" and Lucy's hand clutched mine.

I looked at her. She was right with the film. Her mouth and eyebrows moved and the light from the screen was shining in her face. She was so beautiful that I wanted to stare at her until I'd committed her to memory.

Lucy noticed my staring. She gave me a quick glance and squeezed my hand affectionately. I thought, Palms, don't get sweaty!

After the film was over, we stood on the theater steps in an ebb tide of children. They were all singing and acting out their favorite parts.

Lucy said, "That was brilliant!"

"I'm glad you liked it," I said. "What now?"

"Back to the square for the nine-fifteen bus," Lucy said glumly.

"D'you really have to go home so early?"

"Don't look sad, Lights!" Lucy said. "I had to lie my butt off to get here at all."

"Are your parents strict?"

"Got it in one! Mum says if I want to make it as a dancer, I have to work at it, and that means lots of early nights."

We walked on for a bit, and then Lucy said, "You let go of my hand! Don't you like holding hands?"

I said, "Of course I do!" and we linked fingers.

It was a slow walk, like a walk in a dream. Lucy stopped in front of Posh Foxes and showed me a dress she liked.

"It's a bit sparkly and showbiz, isn't it?" I said.

"I'm a sparkly, showbiz sort of person!" She did a perfect curtsy, still holding my hand. If anyone else had done it, embarrassment would have driven me to disappear into my navel, but it didn't matter with Lucy. It didn't look goofy or posey. It was . . . magical, I suppose.

I said, "Am I going to see you again?"

"Yes," said Lucy. "I'm busy tomorrow, but on Thursday I'm in the dance show at the community center. It starts at seven-thirty and you're going to be there."

"I am?"

"Oh, please!" said Lucy. "I might not be able to talk to you because Mum will be with me, but please be there!"

"All right," I said.

We got to the square at ten past nine, and the bus was waiting at the stop. The driver was standing outside, smoking a cigarette.

"Will you be all right on your own?" I said. "Shall I come with you?"

"No," said Lucy.

I said, "What now, then?"

"This," and she went up onto her toes and kissed me.

It was a brief kiss, a favorite-auntie sort of kiss, but her lips felt incredibly hot and soft. She nuzzled into me just long enough for me to feel her pressed against me, and then she stepped back. She said, "I'm not very good, am I?"

"You're amazing," I said.

Lucy said, "I don't know very much. You know— about boys."

"You're still amazing," I said.

The bus driver climbed into his cab and started the engine. Lucy hopped on and sat down next to a window. As the bus pulled away, she smiled and pressed her palm against the glass.

I watched until the bus's taillights dipped out of sight over the crest of Newhouse Hill.

scene III

casey

I was gone. I was high.

For years my parents and teachers had been telling me that adolescence was going to be a time of Big Emotional Problems—I had repetitive strain injury of the ears from listening to them. Well, now I had the big emotional, but there didn't seem to be a problem—it was excellent. Before I'd been Mr. and Mrs. Freeman's only daughter, or a good student, or a teenager; now I was a person. Someone wanted to talk to me and be with me, someone had noticed that I wasn't the same as everybody else, and that made me notice it too.

The morning after I'd been to Pebbly Beach with Dean, I had a mirror-think. I wanted to see if what had happened showed in my face. I hadn't combed my hair or put on any mascara or anything, so the person in the mirror was still *depressingly* me. I turned my head, trying to see myself the way Dean did, but I couldn't. It wasn't the sort of change you can see in a mirror, because it was on the inside.

In the afternoon I had the place to myself. Mum and Dad were out shopping, and Al went to a mate's house for a sleepover. Helen came round after lunch and she was as fizzy as a well-shaken can of Coke. As soon as I opened my front door she said, "I've been out with him!"

"Who?" I said.

"The boy I didn't know," said Helen. "At least, I did know him, but I didn't know I knew him, sort of thing."

"Who is he?" I said.

"Phil," said Helen. "He danced with us at Fozzer's party. He was the one on his own—the tall one with the hair."

"Oh. Not the short, bald one, then?"

Helen rolled her eyes. "No, listen, he's really nice! We went down to Burger King last night and talked for ages! He's . . . er . . . a senior."

"You brazen hussy! I think you only want him for his walker."

Helen gave me the lowdown on Phil, which included a detailed description of how he ate a burger. I listened, but I wasn't really listening. It all seemed like kid stuff, somehow. I'd been going to tell Helen about my date with Dean, only when I got the chance, I didn't.

You know how you're not supposed to touch a butterfly's wings, because if any of the colored stuff rubs off then the butterfly can't fly anymore? That's what Dean and I felt like. I thought it was too private to share with anyone else, and if I tried, I'd damage it in some way.

Helen said, "I'm seeing him again tonight."

"Don't forget to take your paper bag in case you start hyperventilating," I said.

"Oh, that?" Helen shrugged. "I won't be needing it. I don't get uptight around Phil. He's easy to be with." Her eyes went cloudy. "Boys are funny, aren't they?" she said. "I mean, they try to keep their feelings hidden, but they're really obvious."

"I know," I said. "Touching, isn't it?"

Helen left about half-past three. I mooched about listening to records, wishing something would happen. I must have wished too hard, because it did.

The doorbell rang, and when I opened the door, Dean was standing there. His bike was parked on the road outside the front gate, but I hadn't heard him pull up. I felt a big rush of excitement, but then I noticed his eyes. He was staring at me the way he'd stared at the gorilla at Fozzer's party.

I said, "Dean? What—"

"I met a couple of guys who know you last night," said Dean, and his voice was like the slamming of a freezer lid. "Terry and Lee, they said their names were. I told them I was seeing this girl in the twelfth grade at their school, and when I said it was you, they laughed in my face. Why didn't you tell me you're only fifteen?" The way he said "only" told me a lot of things I didn't want to hear. "Why did you let me go on thinking—"

"I'm sorry," I said. "I didn't think it mattered."

"It matters that you lied to me," said Dean.

"I didn't lie to you. I just didn't tell you the truth, that's all."

Dean shook his head, like a dog trying to get rid of something stuck in its teeth. "I had a year of my parents not telling me the truth in Spain," he said.

He was a cold volcano spewing out a glacier that was crushing me. I could only think of one way to make things better, so I said, "I love you."

"Who needs that crap?" said Dean. "I don't want to be loved!"

"Then what do you want?"

"Oh, get real, will you?"

Tears were coming, making everything blurry. I

wanted to hold him, so I pulled him into the hall, closed the front door and wrapped him in my arms.

"This is wrong!" said Dean. "You shouldn't be doing this!"

His words were saying one thing, but his kisses and the way he held me were saying another. All I was sure about was that I wanted him, and that I could make him want me—so I did.

For a while, I wasn't solid. Time ended. Then Dean and I reached a point where you either have to stop or carry on, and I knew we had to stop. Time restarted, my knees came back and I heard next door's kids shouting as they played outside.

I said, "My parents will be back in about ten minutes."

"I'd better go, then," said Dean.

"I'm not letting you go until you tell me you're going to see me again."

Dean looked up at the ceiling and let out a long breath. "I'm not sure that's a good idea."

"Why not?"

Dean closed his eyes and spoke slowly, trying to get me to understand. "There was this girl in Spain. We picked each other up at a nightclub, and then we'd get together every once in a while and . . . you know."

"Yes," I said. "I was nearly there myself just now."

"It was good," said Dean. "I mean, there was no

pressure, no hassle. It was just what it was. I didn't even think about her when she wasn't there. It was like a perfect relationship."

"I want more than that," I said.

"There isn't any more than that."

"I'll take whatever."

Dean looked at me sharply. "D'you mean it?"

"When am I going to see you again?"

Dean was quiet for a long time. I could feel him weighing things up like he weighed a stone in his hand before he skimmed it. "The day after tomorrow. I've got the night off because I'm working New Year's Eve," he said. "There's this guy at work who'll lend me the keys to his flat if I ask him."

"All right," I said.

"Meet me at the shelter at half seven."

"I'll be there."

When Dean had gone, I felt like a bonfire on the morning after Guy Fawkes Day.

I didn't know about love. Being in love means opening yourself to someone else so much that you can get hurt. Before the hurt happens, you've got no idea of how painful it can be, and it's no good other people telling you; the only way you can find out is to go through it.

scene IV

stew

I started to write a poem for Lucy. I got as far as "You are . . ." and then I stopped, because it was all I needed to write. She was; she existed, and I was delirious about it. I thought, If poets are so wired up about life, why do they sit around writing poetry all day when they could be outside getting on with it?

This was the morning after I'd been out with Lucy, while I was still glittering with aftershock and just before I started counting the nanoseconds until I saw her again.

At lunchtime I met Phil at Ted's, which is the café where we'd invented Barf Bag after trying the poached eggs on toast. Ted's was a perfectly ordinary place, but one thing about it had always puzzled me: There was a menu written out in plastic letters on a board that hung over the counter, and under BEVERAGES it said HOT BOUILLON, which made me wonder if anyone ever asked for it cold.

I got to Ted's before Phil and bought myself a cappuccino. All Ted's coffee tasted the same, but I liked the cappuccino because the foam on the top didn't move when I stirred it. It was one of the few dependable things in a constantly changing world. I was halfway through the coffee when Phil came in. He carried a bunch of roses.

"Phil, you shouldn't have!"

"I think you ought to be warned about how difficult it is to walk with a long-stemmed rose up your butt," said Phil.

"Flowery or thorny end first?"

"Don't tempt me," said Phil. "They're for Helen."

I did a cartoon double take and said, "Helen?"

"*Her*," said Phil. "We had our first social engagement last night, and I'm taking her out again tonight."

"What are you going to do with the roses, hide behind them?"

Phil blinked at me slowly, like an offended frog. "I'm going to give them to her. It's a romantic gesture."

"Good for you! What comes next, breaking into her house and leaving a box of chocolates on her dressing table?"

"These roses have got really long, sharp thorns, you know."

He went to buy himself a cup of coffee, and when he came back I said, "So what's Helen like?"

"A damned sight better than the coffee in this place."

"Is she as good as a deep-pan pizza with extra pepperoni and mozzarella?"

"Too soon to tell," said Phil, "but she's made me buy a bunch of roses, so she must have something."

"Let's hope it's not a pollen allergy," I said.

Phil groaned, sipped his coffee and winced, "It's quite sad, really. I set out to be a True Original, and now I'm just another adolescent cliché. I'm not even sure how it happened."

"Just enjoy," I said.

Phil raised an eyebrow and peered at me suspiciously. "I don't mean to be offensive or anything, but you're happy, aren't you?"

"Yup."

"Is it because you've stopped torturing yourself, or because someone else has started to do it for you?"

"I stopped dreaming and did something," I said. "I think it's working out."

Phil offered me the bunch of roses. "Want to borrow some of these?"

Later on that afternoon I bought a ticket for the show at the community center. There was a poster for it outside, and when I read Lucy's name it gave me a kick inside. I thought, That's *my* Lucy!

And that gave me a kick as well.

Strictly speaking, I'd lied to Phil, because I hadn't stopped dreaming. In fact, I spent the next forty-eight hours dreaming. Some of the dreams overflowed my head and filled the sky: Lucy smiling; Lucy laughing with blossoms in her hair; Lucy in a floaty white dress, standing on tiptoe to kiss me again.

Meanwhile, I walked around, had meals, talked to my family—but don't ask me what I talked about or what I ate, because I haven't got a clue.

When I got to the community center for the dance show, all the front-row seats were reserved. I settled for a seat in the sixth row. I sat next to the aisle, so that if someone tall sat in front of me I could lean to my right and still get a good view.

There was a good turnout. Either more people were interested in dance than I'd thought, or they were all desperate to get away from the TV after being trapped in front of it over Christmas.

It was better than the school concert. It started with the inevitable toddlers. There were about twenty of them dressed as flowers, tottering about the stage while everybody went "Aaw!" I smiled at them so much that it made my teeth go cold.

Next came a free-form dance set in a jungle. The dancers wore animal costumes. The lighting was excellent and I missed the end of the dance because I was trying to make out what kind of lights they were using.

After that, I stopped pretending that I was watching the show and got down to some serious waiting.

Lucy had a solo at the beginning of the second half—a ballet piece with cello accompaniment. When she walked onstage, serene and graceful, my insides came unsprung. When she danced, she took all the light and the attention of the audience and turned it into magic. The music was sad and made me ache, and Lucy was so good that it sent chills down my back.

She danced in the finale too. It was supposed to be an old Hollywood routine with a huge chorus. Lucy played Ginger Rogers to someone else's Fred Astaire. She was wearing a long gray satin dress and she made it flow like liquid. It was breathtaking.

As I watched her glide across the stage, something dawned on me. It wasn't my Lucy up there—not the Lucy who loved Disney movies and curtsied in the middle of High Street. The rest of the dancers were scurrying to get all their moves in, but Lucy could make time stretch to fit her.

At the end of the number there was genuinely enthusiastic applause, and Lucy loved it. She looked around the audience like a daisy turning its head to find the sun. It was a bit depressing, because I'd wanted to keep her to myself, but she was everybody's Lucy. Lucy the Star.

I clapped along with the rest, knowing I'd seen something special, and then I think Lucy spotted me. She raised one hand, palm outward, in just the same way that she'd put her hand up to the bus window.

I'd planned to hang around outside and try to catch a few words with her, but as I left the community center I knew it wouldn't be right. I didn't belong to the world I'd just seen Lucy in.

I felt like the tin soldier who falls in love with a paper ballerina in that fairy story.

scene V

I had a dead weird dream. I was in my bedroom, tidying my wardrobe, and I found a shelf that wasn't normally there. On the shelf was a big pile of sandwiches, all with one bite taken out of them. In the dream, I knew they were mine but I didn't remember putting them away. I felt guilty about taking a bite from each sandwich and then stashing it so I could taste the next one, instead of finishing what I'd started.

When I woke up, I was careful with myself. I explored my feelings like I was checking out a new bruise, not pressing too hard in case it hurt. If I'd been happy or sad, I could have done something about it, but I was in the waiting room, and I wasn't going to find out whether I was happy or sad until after my appointment with Dr. Dean.

I got up, and it was Zombie Girl from Limbo time. I picked all the saddest songs from my CD collection and played them loud—they were the soundtrack for the film of my life.

Helen rang, full of her second date with Phil. He'd been promoted from just plain nice to World's Most Fabulous Human Being. I zombie-talked my way through the conversation.

"Are you all right?" said Helen.

I said, "Sure."

"Only, you don't sound very happy for me."

"Of course I am!" It was myself I wasn't happy for.

"We all ought to get together!" said Helen. "You and Dean, me and Phil."

"Yeah, we must. Sometime."

I didn't tell her about the problems with Dean, because I didn't want to party-poop on her happiness. Also, I was so jealous it hurt. Helen had always had loads of hangups about boys and was really clumsy and shy around them. Now she was Little Miss Sunshine, all bright and confident, and it looked like I was going to wind up asking her for advice. I'd been agony aunt for

Helen's problem of the week for ages. Now it was the other way round.

That was a lonely day. I couldn't even talk to myself because I wasn't there. I called for Casey and she'd moved without letting me know where she was going.

When my parents came home I tried to act normal. I thought I was making a good job of it, but all through dinner Dad kept giving me fatherly looks. He fiddled it so that Mum and Al got to clear the table and load the dishwasher, and when we were on our own he said, "It isn't easy, Casey."

"What isn't?" I said.

"Being a parent," said Dad. "There's no script. I have to make it up as I go along."

"So what's your problem?"

"I understand. Sometimes I can see something's wrong, but if I try to help, you think I'm sticking my nose in."

"It's better that way. If you were too understanding I wouldn't want to leave home, and then you'd be stuck with me for life."

"I already am," said Dad.

I had a really freaky feeling. You know how people who make wildlife films aren't supposed to interfere with the animals they film? I thought my parents were being like that with me. It was freaky because it meant that right when I was in something I figured they'd never be able to understand, they knew exactly what was going on. *I* was the one who didn't understand.

I got ready to go out. I put on the same clothes I'd worn to Fozzer's party. I even wore the same color lipstick. I wanted to remind Dean of the first time we met, and I was also hoping that I could make the magic happen again.

While I waited at the shelter loads of stuff went through my mind. I thought, This is it! I'm going to do *it*.

I remembered just about every dirty joke I'd ever heard, and how I'd laughed at them, trying to pretend that sex was funny, and that the sooner virginity was out of the way, the better. There were girls in ninth grade who'd Gone All the Way, and though most of the other girls talked about them as if they were sluts, secretly they were curious. They'd gather round the ones who'd had sex, going "What's it like?" Now I was going to find out for myself.

And all of a sudden I wasn't a tough little cookie at all. I was scared.

I heard a motorbike and saw Dean pull round the corner into St. Mary's Avenue. He stopped the engine, took off his helmet and looked at me.

I couldn't move from the bench where I was sitting. In my head there was a picture of me getting up, running over to him and hugging him, but I knew that my legs wouldn't work if I tried it.

Dean frowned and said, "Well, are you just going to sit there?"

I didn't know what to do. I wanted to go to him, and I didn't want to. I couldn't work out which was stronger.

"I can't," I said.

"Can't what?" said Dean.

"I can't go with you to the flat."

Dean rolled his eyes and hissed through his teeth. "Great! That's just great!"

"I didn't mean to—"

"No. People never mean to let you down, but they go ahead and do it anyway, don't they?"

His voice was really nasty. It made me want to curl myself up into a ball and roll away. I said, "I'm still that girl you took to Pebbly Beach," in this really pathetic voice.

"No you're not," said Dean. "You're a nice girl who fancied a bit of rough, and now you're chickening out."

And I couldn't say anything, because it was true. That's when I realized now stupid I'd been. I'd made myself believe that Dean and I had something special, but what it came down to was that he wanted sex with no commitment, and I didn't.

I said, "I'm not ready for this."

Dean looked at me like I was a stranger he didn't like very much. "You'll never be ready," he said. "You're a nice girl from a nice family, and you want everything to be perfect and pretty, don't you?"

"Is that so wrong?"

Dean flipped his hair back over his ears and said, "Well, if you won't come to the flat with me, I know someone who will."

"What?"

Dean looked surprised. "You didn't think you were the only one, did you?" He laughed. "You've got a lot of growing up to do, kid."

Dean said it just like a bad actor in some corny film, and I saw that all the hard-man stuff I'd been taken in by was a con, designed to impress people like me.

"Is that all you want me for?" I said.

"It's all anybody wants anybody else for," said Dean.

"I don't believe that."

Dean shrugged. "Suit yourself." He put his helmet back on. Just before he flipped down the visor, he said, "Have a nice life."

"Can't you think of a more original exit line than that?"

"You're not worth it." He started up the bike and rode away.

I sat on the bench for an hour, listening to the

town hall clock chiming the quarters. I was freezing cold and dying for a pee, but I stayed where I was. I could see things clearly, and I wanted to think them through.

You can be in love with being in love. You can get so hooked on the excitements and bliss-outs that even the unhappy parts can be incredibly self-indulgent. When you get like that, you don't love somebody else at all— it's what you've found out about yourself that you're in love with. I'd been so busy mirror-thinking that I'd blown it. The First Great Love of My Life had fallen apart before it had really started.

I got invited to loads of New Year's Eve parties, but I didn't go to any of them. I was afraid I might bump into Dean, and anyway, I wasn't in a party mood. I was convalescing. So I stayed in on New Year's Eve, watching telly with my parents. Al drank two cans of lager, was completely obnoxious for twenty minutes and then crashed out in an armchair. When he started snoring, Mum woke him up and nagged him to bed.

At ten to twelve Dad popped a bottle of sparkling white wine, and when midnight came we toasted in the new year. The telly was showing pictures of people in Trafalgar Square jumping in the fountains and going bananas. It was like the whole world was happy except me.

Dad said, "Happy New Year, Casey." He kissed me on the cheek and gave me a hug.

It was the hug that did it. I went from being a cool teenager in control to a tearful, sobbing wreck. I cried out all the hurt and dead dreams—and most of all, the embarrassment at having got things so wrong.

Dad just held me and didn't say a word.

scene VI

It was the mail slot that changed my life, or at least, the two things that came through the mail slot.

The first thing was a postcard. The writing said, "Please, please, please, please, please—Square. 7 o'clock. Luv, Lucy." On the front was a picture of three ballet dancers in blue tutus. The picture was fuzzy, as though the artist had wanted to cast a glamorous glow over the dancers and their world. Very Lucy. I imagined her writing it, and I noticed how hard she'd pressed with her pen. Her handwriting was looped and loose, just like a girl's, but her name was upright, with a flourish underneath. It was the signature of someone who knew who she was and where she was going.

The second thing was the local free paper. I was walking through the hall when it arrived. I picked it up to immediately toss it in the recycling bin; then I saw a picture of Lucy on the front page. It must have been taken at the community center, because she was in her Ginger Rogers dress.

It gave me a shock of pleasure to see the picture, but then my eyes drifted over to the headline: LOCAL GIRL IS TOPS! I read the article underneath.

Local schoolgirl Lucy Dixon (15) has won a scholarship to the prestigious National College of Dance in London. Lucy came top out of 150 entrants, and is eager to take her place at the college in January. Her dance tutor, Eleanor Deacon . . .

The rest of the article was about outstanding talent and bright futures, and I wasn't in it anywhere.

The rest of the day I was Doomed Love. I saw myself standing on the edge of the cliffs at Pebbly Beach with the wind howling in my ears and the sea crashing onto the rocks far below. I saw myself wandering down wet streets at night, following a ghost who wasn't there.

I thought, I should have known. It was inevitable. I'm one of life's losers, so nothing's ever going to go right for me.

By five o'clock I was restless; by six, I couldn't stand myself anymore. I was too big for the house and I had to get out. I took a long stroll through town and I noticed how depressing Christmas decorations can be. I didn't walk slowly enough, though. I got to the square at ten to seven, and there was nothing to do but soak myself in self-pity. By the time Lucy stepped off her bus, I was well marinated.

When she saw me, her face lit up. She bounded toward me like a puppy that wants to play, and then she noticed the expression on my face. Her feet slowed down, then stopped, and her brightness went out. She stood two yards away, and it was like a thousand years of silence between us. She said, "You know."

"I read about it in the paper," I said.

Lucy bit her bottom lip and said, "Damn!"

"Why didn't you tell me?"

"I was going to, now. That's why I wanted to meet you. I thought I couldn't have passed, then they rang up and said . . ." She ducked her head, trying to get round what I'd put in my eyes. "Please don't look like that, Lights," she said. "I couldn't have done it without you."

"Oh?"

"The audition was the day after you took me out," said Lucy. "I had to dance a piece about a girl who's just fallen in love. If it hadn't been for you, I couldn't have done it properly. I mean, I would have put my feet in the right place, but I wouldn't have understood what it meant."

"Nice to know I was of some use!" I said sarcastically.

Lucy looked alarmed. "You mustn't think . . . !" she said; then she sighed. "I thought you'd never notice me. I noticed you when I was in sixth grade. You were outside the library at school, and you were laughing at something, and I thought . . ." Her words ran out and she shuffled her feet as though she wanted to dance what she meant. "I even went through a phase of following you round—you know, hanging about the places I knew you went. I knew it was only a stupid crush, but it wouldn't go away."

I groaned for all the wasted time and missed chances, and all the energy I'd put into dreams and fantasies. Lucy launched herself at me and gave me a fierce hug. Her hair was in my face and I could smell her skin. I said, "Oh, Dance! I wish you'd said something before!"

I leant back to look at her beautiful, sad face and I felt everything well up inside me. I was going to tell her I loved her, but Lucy said, "Don't say anything."

"Why not?"

"It'll make things more difficult than they already are." She kissed me. It was wishing, waiting and losing, and it meant more than any kiss I'd ever had.

Lucy said, "Let's walk. Talk to me."

"What about?"

"Everything," said Lucy. "I want to know everything. Tell me about what it would have been like."

"What?"

"You and me."

We walked along the side of the square toward Churchill Gardens, and I dreamed out loud. It was mad and painful, but there was something horribly fascinating about it. I told her about sharing a bag of chips at the amusement park and meeting her on the seafront at Pebbly Beach, and playing her all my favorite CDs.

We turned into St. Mary's Avenue and I noticed another couple on the other side of the road. The bloke was standing next to a motorcycle and the girl was sitting on one of the benches by the park shelter. She was hanging on every word he was saying. It looked like they were actually having a relationship, not just talking about it.

We passed St. Mary's church and Lucy pulled me into a back lane away from the streetlights. I don't know how many times we kissed. Lucy kept on saying, "Is this what it would have been like?" and I said,

"Yes," and for a while it was. For a while we were able to hold the future at arm's length, but then our time ran out, and the future was still there.

"Will you write to me?" said Lucy.

"I don't know."

"Will you come and see me in London?"

"It wouldn't be any good," I said. "We'd be thinking about saying goodbye all the time."

We were already thinking about it. We went back into the street and walked nowhere.

"D'you know what I did yesterday afternoon?" Lucy said. "I read through some of the ballet school books I bought when I was in elementary school, and I thought, I'm really going there. I'm really going to do it!"

I could imagine her hair falling over the page, her face pulling exactly the same expressions as when she was watching the Disney movie. I think that's when I first realized the difference between the real Lucy and the fantasy girl in my head—real Lucy had dreams and ambitions of her own, and she wasn't about to throw them away because of me.

We got to the bus and Lucy turned to me. "Are you going to see me again before I leave?"

"No," I said.

Lucy frowned. "Are you going to kiss me goodbye?"

"I can't. You've already gone."

"If things were different . . . ," said Lucy, and then she stopped, because things weren't going to be different. "I'm sorry."

"There's nothing to be sorry for," I said. "It's not your fault." When I said it, it was to make Lucy feel better about going; after it was said, I realized that it was true.

As the bus drove away, I stuck my hands in my pockets and my right knuckles knocked against something cold and hard. It was the fossil I'd picked up on Pebbly Beach, the one I'd meant to give Lucy. I went to put it in the litter bin near the bus stop, but then I thought, No. You keep this and remember, although I already knew I was never going to forget.

I don't know who said "'Tis better to have loved and lost than never to have loved at all," but he was the biggest liar who ever lived.

scene VII

casey

ı was looking forward to the new term. The one thing to be said for schoolwork is that if you actually do it, it takes your mind off other things. I thought it was time for a new Casey, the conscientious student who took herself and her education seriously.

Trouble was, when I got back to school it was exactly the same as when I left. Mrs. Pereira still couldn't control our Spanish class and the causes of the First World War still gave me grief.

At lunchtime I gave Helen edited highlights of the

Dean thing. In this version I'd been really cool and mature and decided that neither of us was ready for a serious relationship. I made out that I'd cracked our hearts to avoid breaking them.

Helen was impressed. Her eyes went shiny and she said, "You sacrificed yourself for love!"

I said, "Er, yeah. Well, you do, don't you?"

"I know!" said Helen. "I'd sacrifice myself for Phil if I had to." She made it sound like any minute she was going to be dragged off by the Inquisition and burned at the stake. "In fact, I've already made a sacrifice for him. I've stopped worrying about my bum."

"Whoo-whee! Keep a grip, Hel!"

"Phil likes me just the way I am," she said.

Mental note: It's possible to meet someone who makes you feel good about yourself. It doesn't have to be about tears and suffering.

Last lesson was English. Mr. Hart handed out our new text for the term, *A Midsummer Night's Dream*, and did his best to get us warmed up about Shakespeare.

I said, "Why are we reading a play about Midsummer Night in the middle of winter?"

"It's not about summer," said Mr. Hart. "It's about people who fall in love with the wrong people and all the complications it causes."

I thought, Oh, really? Tell me about it!

I hung round at the end of the lesson and when everybody else had gone, I went up to Mr. Hart and said, "Can I talk to you?"

"Other than which there is almost nothing else I'd rather do, Casey," said Mr. Hart.

I took a deep breath and said, "I had one of those love affairs you recommended. They hurt, don't they?"

Mr. Hart looked distressed. "Oh, God, I hope you didn't get into anything painful because of what I said to you. I'd hate to think that—"

"It was my fault," I said. "Can I borrow a piece of chalk?"

I went into *Dean II, The Director's Cut*, and it was a lot more truthful than what I'd told Helen. While I was talking, I drew a picture of my life on the board, with a big spiral for Dean and jagged lines for the pain. I put in Mum and Dad, Helen and Phil, the benches at Churchill Park and the waves on Pebbly Beach.

Mr. Hart was good—I mean, I was a bit jokey about the hurt, but I could see in his eyes that he could tell how deep it went. Talking to him helped because I had to put all the pieces together, and when I finished I saw how they fitted.

Mr. Hart said, "I had bad times when I was your age, Casey. I wouldn't do the years between fifteen and twenty-two again for anything."

"What happened to you when you were twenty-two?"

"I met my wife," said Mr. Hart. "When I did, it all made sense. She reminded me of everyone I'd had a relationship with before. I think I must have fallen in love with bits of her that were in other people. Relationships are like stepping-stones."

"They *are*?"

"Sure! Every relationship is another stepping-stone on the way to where you're going. You've got to step from one stone to the next because there aren't any shortcuts, but each step you take you're getting closer."

"Closer to what?"

"Finding out what makes you happy," said Mr. Hart.

"But I screwed it up! I was so stupid!"

"You're only stupid if you don't learn from it," said Mr. Hart. "You can't expect to be an expert the first time round."

I thought, Hey! Optimism!

"Thanks, Mr. Hart. You're a pretty OK guy, you know?"

"Well, that's good, Casey, because you're a pretty OK guy yourself." Then he gave me this funny frown and smile. "Do me a favor, will you?"

"What?" I said.

"Come and see me for a chat tomorrow after school."

"Cool," I said. Just before I left, I turned for a final glance at the picture of my life. It was a total mess.

I thought about what Mr. Hart had said, and I knew things would be all right in the end. I still hurt about Dean, but now I could see a point to that hurt. I'd been there, done that, bought the T-shirt and I wasn't going to buy it again. No one goes over stepping-stones backward.

I wanted to do something to thank Mr. Hart properly, so I made him a card. On the front, I drew this big red heart with legs, and inside I put THANK YOU. LOADSA LUV, CASEY XO, which wasn't the most witty or original message in the world, but at least it was sincere.

When I went to see Mr. Hart at the end of the school the next day he was talking to this senior guy. I hung around in the corridor for a bit, and I was just going to slink off when Mr. Hart waved me into his room. "Casey!" he said. "Did you want to see me about something?"

"No, you told me to—"

"Sorry!" Mr. Hart interrupted. "Can't stay—staff meeting! But there's someone here I think you should meet. Stewart, this is Casey. Casey, this is Stewart."

Stewart blushed and said, "Hello!"

I half recognized him. I'd seen him around somewhere, but I couldn't place him.

As Mr. Hart was leaving, he leaned close and whispered, "He needs to talk to someone. Not a happy lad, is Stewart."

"Why?" I said.

"Guess," said Mr. Hart.

I looked at Stewart, and this time I saw LOVE PROBLEMS stamped all over him. "What can I do?" I said.

"Your best," said Mr. Hart. "And be gentle with him."

"But . . . ?"

"Bye!" said Mr. Hart.

I thought, Oh, cheers, Mr. Hart, dumping me here with a complete stranger and expecting me to sort him out! Thanks a lot, mate!

Stewart cleared his throat, put his hands in his pockets and then took them out again. He looked as awkward as I felt. I didn't know how to go about starting a conversation with him, but I've never been one for creeping around the back stairs. I'm more a kick-down-the-front-door type.

"Has some girl been giving you a hard time, then?"

"No," said Stewart. "One particular girl has been giving me a hard time."

"Join the club. Love sucks, doesn't it?"

Stewart laughed. It was a good laugh, the kind that makes you want to join in, so I did.

"D'you know Lucy Dixon?" asked Stewart.

"That's where I've seen you before! Just before

Christmas! You came out of Burger King with this other guy and then . . ."

"Yes," agreed Stewart. "Well, the thing is . . ."

He told me about it. I thought it would be so boring that I'd have to stick my pencil in my arm to stay awake, but it was pretty interesting. Stewart had a bit of a thing for words, and he could tell the story like I'd actually been there with him; plus the fact that I knew where he was coming from because I was in the same place myself. And while he was talking, I noticed him. Sometimes when you first meet people you don't notice what they look like, and then they do something and you really see them. With Stewart it was his eyes. They were kind of soft, and you could look right through them to what was going on inside him.

I thought, Hang on! This bloke is trusting you! and it was weird, because I wanted to trust him back. One part of me was going, Whoa there! You hardly know this guy! and another part of me felt like we were going to be really good mates.

It got dark and we left the classroom, heading for home. We wound up by the tennis courts. I said, "I didn't know boys were like that."

"Like what?" said Stewart.

"Sort of sensitive and . . ."

"Sappy? I'm good at sappy. I sometimes think it's the only thing I'm good at."

"I don't know. You're good at talking."

"Ah, but you should try my listening! I turn into a huge ear that you can bend."

"Fancy a coffee?" I said. "My house is just down the road."

It wasn't like I cared if he said yes or no, but it was freezing cold and it was comforting to meet someone who was in as much of a mess as I was.

"Yes, I'd like to if that's all right."

"It's going to cost you," I said.

"Oh?"

"I'm going to bend that famous ear of yours."

On the way to the house, I hit Stewart with *Dean III, Return to Heartbreak*. This time it was different. You know how when you tell a joke there comes a point when it freezes in your mind, so you always use exactly the same words whenever you tell the joke again? That's what happened to the story of Dean and me. I told it the way I was always going to tell it, and it suddenly felt like it had happened a long time ago when I was someone different.

Over coffee we talked about a lot of other stuff. Stewart turned out to be Helen's Phil's best mate, and his favorite place in the world was Pebbly Beach, and I was just about to go, Hey! It's *The Creepy Coincidence Show*! when Mum came in from work.

Stewart was really sweet when he met Mum. He

shook hands and said how pleased he was to meet her, and he was like a polite little boy. We chatted for a bit longer, but you know how it is—you can't get deep and meaningful with a parent in the room.

I saw Stewart to the door, and he said, "Thanks, Casey. I really needed that talk."

"The feeling's mutual."

"If it ever gets bad—about Dean, I mean—you can always give me a call, or something."

"Same goes for you if it gets bad about Lucy."

We swapped phone numbers, and then Stewart left.

After I shut the door, I turned round and Mum was in the kitchen doorway with her interested face on. "He's new, isn't he?" she said.

"He's been telling me about his girl troubles."

"Quite nice, isn't he?" said Mum.

I had to think about the answer to that. I thought about Stewart's eyes, and the way he laughed, and how the last couple of hours had felt. "Yeah," I said. "Stewart's all right."

In fact, when I came to think about it, I liked Stewart quite a lot.

epilogue

stew

Before I met casey I was dark blue; afterward I was more of a pale turquoise.

We met by accident . . . I think.

When I got back to school after the holidays, I was desperate for someone to talk to. Frank had gone back to university early, and Phil was so besotted with Helen, I couldn't get any sense out of him. Lucy was still an open wound and I needed someone to help me bandage it up, so at the end of the first day, I went to see Mr. Hart. I'd picked the wrong time because he was talking to Casey—though I didn't know it was Casey then. She was babbling away, drawing on the blackboard, and she didn't see me in the corridor. Mr. Hart did, though, because he raised his eyebrows to tell me he couldn't talk right then, and then something happened in his face. He glanced at Casey, looked back at me, and smiled.

I thought, He's flipped! Another victim of Teacher Burnout.

I was even more convinced Mr. Hart had flipped the following day. He sent a message via my homeroom teacher telling me to come and see him in his room at the end of school. When I did, Mr. Hart said, "Ah, Stewart! I'm glad you came. Sorry about the message, but I completely forgot that there's a staff meeting tonight—or detention for teachers, as we call it."

I said, "Oh." I felt pretty down. I'd been hoping to unburden myself about Lucy in front of Mr. Hart's sympathetic audience, but now the chance had been snatched away. I thought, It figures. When I really need to see people, they're not available.

Mr. Hart leaned close and said confidentially, "See that girl out in the corridor?"

I said, "The skinny one who's hopping about?"

"Talk to her," said Mr. Hart.

"Me?" I said. "Why?"

"No time to explain, just do it," said Mr. Hart; then he called Casey in and introduced us.

I recognized her, because I'd seen her talking to Mr. Hart, so I knew she was one of his flock of lame ducks.

Mr. Hart went to the staff meeting and left Casey and me alone together. I didn't know what to say, but then Casey said, "Has some girl been giving you a hard time, then?" She was like a ram-raider coming through a plateglass window; not so much direct as brutal.

I can't remember what I said after that, but Casey said something that made me laugh, and she laughed too, and when we stopped I noticed how sad she was. It wasn't a wistful sort of sadness, but a dark, broody one—thundercloud sadness. I thought, So, you think *you're* sad? I'll show you *sad*!

And I talked about Lucy.

The talk went into the corridor, out through the doors of the school and along the path that ran past the tennis courts. My story was a poignant tragedy of happiness snatched away at the very point of being realized. Casey listened with her eyes big and round for the happy parts, narrow and sympathetic for the despair. When I finished, I paused, expecting her to murmur something consoling.

"Sheesh!" she said. "What a bummer!"

It cracked me up. I laughed so hard, I was afraid I

might cry. It was funny, because Casey had summed it up so neatly. Maybe there would be Life After Lucy, so long as I didn't take it too seriously.

"Mr. Hart says you learn from all this stuff," said Casey.

"Learn what?" I said.

"How to do it better."

"What, getting hurt?"

"No!' said Casey. "Just remember, every stepping-stone has a silver lining."

I didn't understand her, and I didn't try because I noticed how dark it was. The streetlights were on and it made me realize how much of Casey's time I'd taken up. I was trying to think of a way to say goodbye, but it was difficult because I didn't want to—talking to Casey was fun.

Then, right out of the blue, Casey said, "Fancy a coffee? My house is just down the road," and I was saved. I said yes like a shot.

On the way, Casey told me her story, and suddenly it was a game of emotional I'll Show You Mine if You'll Show Me Yours. Long before she reached the end, I could tell what Casey's problem had been. She'd been going out with a bloke called Dean, and he was all moody darkness, while she was sparklers.

"You don't need someone who's a challenge!" I said. "You don't have to prove anything."

"I know that now," said Casey, "but I didn't know it before."

"You need a bit of romance," I said.

Casey screwed up her nose. "Get outta here! You need someone who'll keep your feet on the ground, mate!"

Right that moment, it felt like I'd known Casey for years. I'd forgotten it was possible to like someone—just plain like, with no entanglements. I smiled at Casey, and she smiled back . . . and then it was time to leave, because her mother came in.

Casey and I exchanged phone numbers before I went. It was my idea. I said if she ever felt down she could call me, and she said the same. Afterward, I wished that I'd told her she could call me anytime, not just for therapy, but it didn't occur to me until it was too late.

As I was walking home, it suddenly struck me that I'd actually talked to a girl for about two and a half hours without getting clumsy or shy. I'd said far more to Casey than I'd ever said to Lucy, because in a way I hadn't wanted to talk to Lucy at all. I'd just wanted to watch her being perfect—Lucy, the Unattainable Star. In fact, *all* the girls I'd fallen in love with had been un-attainable, because unattainable meant safe. Never being able to get close meant never being disappointed or disillusioned, and no pain other than a massive wallow in self-pity.

Casey was something else. She was loud and funny and outrageous . . . and real. You couldn't possibly make Casey into something she wasn't, because she'd kick you in the shins if you so much as tried. I kept thinking of something she'd said about every stepping-stone having a silver lining. It still didn't make any sense, but the image was nice—a deep stream, studded with mossy stones, and in the water round each stone, a circle of glittering light. The stones were wet and slippery and dangerous, but the silver linings made them irresistibly beautiful.

The picture got me thinking deeper. Sometimes, when you think you're ready for something, you're wrong and right at the same time; you're right about being ready, but wrong about what you're ready for. Casey had been wrong about Dean the way I'd been wrong about Lucy—but I was ready for something; I could feel it. Maybe it was already happening, and I didn't know it yet.

Another day, another stepping-stone.

about the
author

Andrew Matthews was born in Wales in 1948.
He wrote his first story when he was seven years old
and had so much fun that he forgot to stop writing.
After a career as a high school English teacher, he became a full-time writer in 1994. Since then he has written more than fifty books, many of which have been
translated into foreign languages.

Andrew Matthews lives in Reading, near London,
with his wife, Sheena, and their cats. When he is working, the cats help by sitting on his notebooks, hiding
his pens and walking over his keyboard. When he is
not working, Andrew enjoys crosswords, reading, listening to music and watching movies. He is a member
of the UK Wolf Conservation Trust and has scratched a
wolf's stomach.